Christmas 1987.

To Terry,
from Mom & Dad 2
with love

From the Heart   Folk Art in Canada

Canadian Centre for Folk Culture Studies of the National Museum of Man

From the Heart

Folk Art in Canada

McClelland and Stewart

in cooperation with the

National Museum of Man   National Museums of Canada

CANADIAN CATALOGUING IN PUBLICATION DATA

Main entry under title:
From the heart: folk art in Canada

Issued also in French under title: Du fond du coeur.
Catalogue of an exhibition held at the Glenbow
Museum, Calgary, Alberta, Mar. 7-May 2, 1983,
and other museums.

ISBN 0-7710-9021-8 (bound)
ISBN 0-7710-9022-6 (pbk.)

1. Folk art—Canada—Exhibitions. 2. Art industries
and trade—Canada—Exhibitions. I. Canadian Centre
for Folk Culture Studies. II. Glenbow Museum.

NK 841.F 76   745'.0971'074   C83-094005-7
SCC Catalogue No. NM92-88/1983E

Édition française:
Du fond du coeur—L'art populaire au Canada
Relié: ISBN 0-660-90272-9
Broché: ISBN 0-660-90273-7
Publié par les Musées nationaux du Canada

The Canadian publishers:

McClelland and Stewart Limited
25 Hollinger Road, Toronto M4B 3G2
in cooperation with the
National Museum of Man
National Museums of Canada
Ottawa, Canada K1A 0M8

From the Heart:
Folk Art in Canada
was written by
Jean-François Blanchette,
Magnus Einarsson,
Stephen Inglis,
Wesley Mattie and
Philip Tilney,
under the direction of
Pierre Crépeau,
chief of the Canadian Centre
for Folk Culture Studies

PRINTED AND BOUND IN HONG KONG
BY SCANNER ART SERVICES INC TORONTO

Contents

Foreword

The Allstate Foundation, with its objectives of advancing and supporting the social and cultural spirit of the Canadian community, takes great pride in sponsoring the exhibition "From the Heart: Folk Art in Canada". From the beginning, our interest in the project was sparked by the strength of these intuitive and unselfconscious works of art. Their beauty communicates on a human scale the connection that exists between people and their traditions and does so in a way that is especially moving.

This exhibition came about through the expertise and dedication of a number of people, but our particular thanks go to Dr. William E. Taylor, Jr., Director of the National Museum of Man, National Museums of Canada. In addition, we offer our special appreciation to Linda McKnight, President, McClelland and Stewart, publishers of this book.

Finally, The Allstate Foundation acknowledges with thanks the talent of the artists, both named and anonymous, whose works are represented here. It is their vision which in the end makes this an extraordinary exhibition. For each individual piece in "From the Heart: Folk Art in Canada" is at its core·a celebration of self-expression that shines, in the words of William Wordsworth, "with the innocent beauty of a newborn day."

David B. Winn, *President*
THE ALLSTATE FOUNDATION

Director's Foreword

The National Museum of Man is proud to present this exhibition of Canadian folk art.

"From the Heart: Folk Art in Canada" is eloquent proof that creative genius and artistic talent are not confined to the select few whose works are the pride of art galleries and wealthy collectors. Art is all around us; it is part and parcel of our social and cultural environment. Art brings to life the words and deeds of not only poets and painters, but also farmers, housewives, labourers, and artisans.

This exhibition reveals much about the artists themselves. Behind each work lies a story of tragedy, suffering, fantasy or joy. "From the Heart" provides an opportunity for aesthetic contemplation and a sharing of emotions while presenting the remarkable diversity of our Canadian heritage.

"From the Heart: Folk Art in Canada" was made possible through the cooperation of a great many people. Mention should be made, first of all, of the folk artists represented in this exhibition and of the thousands of others whose works enrich the collections of the National Museum of Man.

The exhibition was organized by the staff of the museum's Canadian Centre for Folk Culture Studies. Jean-François Blanchette, Magnus Einarsson, Stephen Inglis, Wesley Mattie and Philip Tilney also wrote the catalogue under the direction of Pierre Crépeau, Chief of the Centre.

Welcome outside advice was received from Paul Carpentier, Gerald Ferguson, J. Russell Harper, Thomas Lackey, Jean Simard and David Thauberger. Innumerable artists and their families, collectors, and fellow museum workers contributed suggestions and information, notably Louis Bolduc, George Hamell, Christopher Huntington, Blake and Ruth McKendry, Ralph and Patricia Price, Raymond Reside, Michael Rowan, and Nettie Sharpe. Warm thanks should go to the Canadian Broadcasting Corporation and Donnalu Wigmore for permission to use their film, *From the Heart*, in connection with the exhibition. We are also deeply appreciative of the on-going support of the Multicultural Directorate of the Department of the Secretary of State.

Finally, we are delighted to record our wholehearted appreciation to The Allstate Foundation of Canada, whose generous sponsorship made this travelling exhibition available across the country.

William E. Taylor, Jr., *Director*
NATIONAL MUSEUM OF MAN

By Way of a Preface

Clem began his working life as a scarecrow, standing patiently in a cornfield, repelling hordes of ravenous birds. But his rather sly demeanour and his obvious delight in life soon attracted the attention of passers-by. One of them, one day, drawn one step closer than the others, took Clem away and showed him the path to immortality.

Because of his humour and charm, Clem was chosen as the exhibition's symbol of Canadian folk artists. He embodies the spirit of all those artists, known and unknown, whose skill, imagination and wry humour knit together the fabric of this vast land. They kindle our wonder with their art, and with the spark of inspiration tell us stories of our past and present and of the times to come.

Introduction

"This is a young country where art and life go hand in hand, for the benefit and happiness of all. Life cannot be beautiful without art, nor art flourish without life." MARIUS BARBEAU ("LES ARTS TRADITIONNELS")

Folk art in Canada reveals a feeling for life, a feeling nurtured by memories, drawn from moments of tenderness, and expressed in the restless stirrings of countless imaginations. Framed by tradition and shaped by experience, the feelings come from the heart, and are shared by us all. Folk art is our art, the reflection of a search for our roots and our destiny—a search that never ends.

When Marius Barbeau brought the first pieces of folk art to the National Museum of Canada in the 1920s, his intention was to direct the attention of Canadians toward the art of the people and to rescue what he regarded as the last vestiges of the traditional arts before they died out. Believing that art "is at home in the shanties of the humble...as well as in the palaces of the great",[1] he travelled throughout Canada looking for works that expressed the creative gifts at work in every group of our complex society. Folksongs, folktales and legends, furniture and sculptures made by craftsmen, the "thousand little skills"[2] were, in his eyes, varied expressions of the arts that embellish life. Barbeau's interest laid the basis for a Canadian Centre for Folk Culture Studies, which supports research not only in folk art, but also into the music, lore and customs of the entire range of Canada's immigrant communities. The emphasis in those early years was on the collection of oral folklore, and it is only in the last decade that the Centre has acquired most of its artifacts, including the collections of several farsighted and dedicated collectors. They include pieces representing traditional art forms that are no longer created as well as ongoing purchases of contemporary works. Following in Barbeau's path, the Centre acquires objects from working artists and takes special care to discern their meaning.

Folk art may be seen as an aspect of the social process, created by people who work in particular physical, social and cultural conditions, and reflecting a collective understanding. What are the motivations of the artists? How did they learn, and what techniques do they use? What are their sources of inspiration? What is their personal history? What is the influence of their natural and social environments? The answers to these questions add a deeper meaning to the appeal of the objects and lead us to a fuller appreciation of folk art.

1   Marius Barbeau, "Les arts traditionnels", in *La Renaissance campagnarde* (Montréal: Albert Lévesque, 1935), p. 52.

2   Marius Barbeau, *Saintes artisanes*, vol. 2, *Mille petites adresses* (Montréal: Fides, 1946).

From the Heart

Both the exhibition and the book are laid out in four sections, the first three designed to illustrate specific themes and characteristics of folk art. Clem is the "preface", the mascot of the exhibition and the elemental symbol of the Canadian folk artist. The three major themes that follow are entitled *Reflection*, *Commitment*, and *Fantasy*. While each of them deals with very different creative impulses, certain elements recur. Fantasy and humour, for example, though highlighted in the third section, crop up frequently throughout the exhibition. In the last section, the work of four Canadian folk artists is presented in some detail, further developing the themes previously presented.

REFLECTION

The exhibition opens with artifacts that represent various aspects of traditional life. They demonstrate the emphasis folk artists place on recording, describing, memorializing and passing on to others images that have become meaningful through experience.

The first objects displayed are tools and other utilitarian objects. A useful tool is an efficient tool, but excellence can also be expressed through artful shape, ornamentation, or complex narrative and symbolic motifs. Homemade tools are often so personalized that they express thoughts, emotions and values. Opening the exhibition with subtly shaped and ornamented tools helps to emphasize that much folk art developed in conjunction with utilitarian needs.

Nature provides folk artists with endlessly diverse sources of inspiration. The handmade decoy, for example, not only promises a successful hunt, but also becomes a source of pleasure to the carver in the likeness achieved. Pride in domestic livestock as well as fascination with animals in the wild have also provided subject-matter to the folk artist. The astonishing variety and elegance of creatures depicted in weather-vanes indicates the sensitivity of the artists to the world of nature. The challenge of rough lands and turbulent seas and the ways in which they were encountered, in reality or fantasy, have been recorded. Through the artist we glimpse the vast expanse and the diversity of Canada, from the sea coasts to the forests and plains, as well as the hardships and the satisfactions experienced in settling here. Through their art, many of these settlers look back to a birthplace far beyond the shores of Canada and reflect on their memories of the Old Country, the pain of leaving, and their hopes for life in the New World.

For the artists whose works are represented in this section, the opportunity to express themselves in this way came only after retirement. Since rapid changes in technology have drastically altered tools and work patterns, many artists recreate the details of their own working lives in miniature. For some the motivation is quiet nostalgia, while for others it is a strong desire to record what life was like and to pass that knowledge on to the young. Images of work and struggle appear side by side with those of recreation and the simpler games and amusements of a bygone era. Some folk artists used leisure time to reflect on their oral traditions and to give material form to tales, legends and other forms of community wisdom.

The folk art of reflection is primarily one of familiarity, of day-to-day experiences accumulated over a lifetime, and of skills and ideals shared within a community.

COMMITMENT

The second section contains folk art created to express commitment. In the art of commitment, the artist, speaking personally or for the community, declares loyalty to other individuals, to nations, social groups or to God. Folk art of this kind is often highly symbolic in nature. Some of these symbols, such as the cross, embrace the Christian community; others, like the Canadian beaver, may represent a nation and embody valued qualities, such as industry and persistence. Some symbols are held in common only within much smaller groups, or have achieved a special meaning for the people of a particular region, such as the schooner and lighthouse motif so common in Maritime folk art. Still another range of artifacts derives its symbolism from a ceremonial occasion or a stage of life, for example the love-spoons given as a sign of betrothal, or a hope chest begun during adolescence. All works of commitment are alike, however, in that they carry an emotional charge beyond their aesthetic content.

Icons are commonly understood to be religious portraits that embody the holiness or power of the sacred personage portrayed. In recent years, however, icons have been spoken of in broader, secular terms, encompassing family or group mementoes. For example, genealogies, commemorative plaques, portraits, patriotic mottoes, and souvenirs from ancestral homelands all fit into this category. These objects share a quality beyond their artistic merit; they capture for the owner the essence of what they depict, evoking feelings of love and reverence.

In Canada, the ethnic icon is of special interest because of the multicultural character of the population and the strong ties that many Canadians retain to their birthplaces. Family icons are usually displayed in a kind of sanctuary, ranging from a single shelf to an entire room. They may vary a great deal in type and artistry, but each piece has an impact beyond that of its actual form. Such icons may be as obvious as a painting or photograph, or as modest as an ashtray or piece of embroidery symbolizing the owner's cultural heritage.

Religion is another aspect of life that is comfortably served by symbols, icons and other objects containing an almost magical power. Religious pictures, crucifixes and statues, as well as simple scriptural admonitions and prayers, have thus long had a prominent place in Canadian homes. The same is true of the non-Christian folk-religious symbols and protective amulets, although they are less widely known. The artistically woven corn dollies made from the last sheaf of the harvest (nos. 134–6), which guarantee the success of next year's crop, fulfil the same function as the lucky four-leaf clover or the horseshoe over the door. Some of these symbols have a dual meaning. The cross, for example, is a symbol of both the sun and the crucified Son of God. The weather-vane cock, among the most commonly used and understood symbols, stands not only for the dawn and the Resurrection, but also for fertility. In essence, these are the symbols that help people to cope with the myriad unfathomable forces in life.

One of the strongest creative forces in Canadian folk art arises from the contemplation of love and sex. Women, in addition to providing everyday wear, have stitched handkerchiefs, pillowcases and quilts with embroidered endearments and pictorial tokens of love, including hearts and flowers, chains and turtle doves. Men, in occupations that took them away from home for months at a time, have fashioned images or messages of various types for their loved ones. Very often these were engagement presents and were modelled on specific traditional forms and patterns, such as the scrimshaw and baleen trinkets made by whalers, or the chip-carved boxes and figurines of isolated woodsmen. Objects such as these, made for a specific person, become powerful tokens of the emotional bond between maker and recipient.

The intention in the making of icons, talismans and tokens of commitment is not primarily aesthetic. Using, or simply contemplating, these affectionate mementoes, for example, may bring a separated couple together for a brief moment. Although the artist frequently calls upon aesthetics to transform absence into felt presence, the object is meaningful not only for its beauty but also for the power of its message.

FANTASY

The third section is devoted to works of imagination, humour and fantasy. Such pieces often represent an intricate venture into the world of whimsy. The artists choose to deal with improbable situations, such as bringing in the hay in bathing suits (no. 187)—an unlikely and itchy proposition—or to express their personal visions, as did a Nova Scotia artist in his carnival rendition of the world (no. 213). Most of the folk art in this exhibition implies adherence to a community tradition, yet many of the fanciful objects in this section are an intricate step beyond these traditions, moving into the realm of unpredictability and innovation. These pieces of whimsy and fantasy come from the mind as well as from the heart.

Whimsy suggests something casual, something tossed off without trying, yet whimsy in folk art is considerably more complex. In a sense the artist is taking a risk, exploring personal ideas and interpretations, and risking the possible shock or alienation of the viewer. Some whimsical pieces, such as a complexly carved chain, may have traditional models but no recognizable function other than to show dexterity. A birdhouse, on the other hand, has a definite function, yet the addition of an aviary garbage can and a hairpin porch railing (no. 221) is prompted by sheer whimsy. This impulse is even more obvious in the concept of two cats dancing sedately to accordion accompaniment (no. 205), or in the unsmiling figure of a go-go dancer with hinged breasts (no. 189).

The undeniable humour in many of these pieces is sometimes subtle and understated. However, the carving of a naked woman feeding a skunk (no. 206) borders on the ludicrous, although it is not unusual in the context of this artist's other bizarre miniatures. Similarly, the tiny carving of a cold lumberjack (no. 184) is unquestionably comic, his puffed-out red cheeks and pursed lips immediately evoking the kind of weather familiar to all Canadians.

In other examples from this section, fantasy is the strongest element, allowing us a glimpse into an inner world of dreams and visions. In some cases, the fantasies are erotic, a world of bathing beauties, caressing and making love. Other fantasies give a glimpse into the artist's private world. Consider the Québec garden filled with huge giraffes and penguins (no. 215); or a large bird painted in pink and green polka dots and carrying a small army of tiny offspring on its broad back (no. 218).

Although traditional carving and painting techniques are used, some of these pieces explore subjects well beyond the range of what is considered traditional. It is perhaps too easy to dismiss this kind of non-traditional creation as personal fantasy, because the conscious motivation of the artists in terms of their traditional backgrounds is unclear. In many cases even the artist is unable or unwilling to offer an explanation. Despite the term *eccentric*, often applied to folk art that does not seem to fit any of the accepted moulds, pieces of personal fantasy and vision appear with increasing frequency in contemporary folk art. Perhaps they have existed all along, and it is only now that we have begun to recognize their importance.

FOLK ARTISTS

The final section provides a detailed examination of the works of four Canadian folk artists.

Nelphas Prévost makes fiddles and cases adorned with figurative and symbolic designs. Many of his carved and painted root-sculptures have been sold or given to his neighbours and to those who come to buy his axe and hammer handles. Sam Spencer's carved plaques, depicting nature scenes and popular images, have accumulated over the years until the walls of his house are covered with them. Frank Kocevar's paintings proclaim his ideals and carry the viewer back through his past; they are the means he found to record his own history. Failing eyesight has done little to restrain George Cockayne's creative imagination. He has continued to turn surplus pieces of wood and other scrap into creations reflecting a personal vision.

The work of each artist illustrates at least one of the themes around which this exhibition has been organized: Prévost, the elaboration of utilitarian objects; Spencer, the depiction of nature; Kocevar, the recording of the past and of images of commitment; and Cockayne, the pursuit of a vision of imagination and fantasy. In addition, the four selected folk artists demonstrate a variety of styles and media, and represent various regions of Canada.

Each of them has a unique approach, yet shares with the other three and with many other artists in the exhibition certain experiences that may be important in reaching an understanding of folk art in Canada today. All four artists are self-taught; they have rural backgrounds and have worked hard for a living; all of them are fond of the outdoors and feel a special rapport with nature; each works alone but is inspired by the interest of other people in his work; and each shows determination and a deep satisfaction in creativity.

Folk Art in Transition

The folk aesthetic traditions of Canada were first developed within defined ethnic and cultural groups all over the globe. In addition to the native peoples, these groups included the early settlers from Europe and the immigrants who came later from every corner of the world. Today, as folk art in Canada moves gradually away from the tastes and conventions of those original traditions, a single piece may reflect various influences as well as express a personal impulse. Modern works tend to reflect the blending of cultural traditions and particular regional characteristics as often as they represent their creators' origins.

Folk art has often been characterized as conformist in nature and essentially utilitarian. It has long been viewed only as a traditional art, its links with the past emphasized to the neglect of the present. The artists have been seen as people whose artistic limits seem to be reached in the ornamentation of everyday objects like tools, furniture and textiles. Such interpretations of the folk artist may date back to the quickening of nationalism in nineteenth-century Europe, when in the Romantic view of the period peasants were perceived as the custodians of the national soul.

Recently, however, this view has changed. Those with an interest in folk art no longer look only to the past, for contemporary works of folk art can be as aesthetically pleasing and can provide as meaningful a perspective. Much folk art, in fact, reflects the rapidly changing nature of Canadian society. Folk artists are no longer always anonymous and submerged in the conservative traditions of their communities. More and more folk artists emerge as articulate individuals, able to explain their aims and motivations themselves. As a result, several tendencies in contemporary folk art can be readily identified.

FROM TRADITION TO INNOVATION

The first tendency is revealed in the movement from tradition to innovation. Folk art has been distinguished by the retention of techniques, forms, symbols and motifs inherited from the past and transmitted from generation to generation by a succession of artists. However, contemporary folk artists tend to innovate on the technical level, as well as in their use of symbols and motifs. The design of homemade sugar moulds (nos. 150–58), for example, was restricted by recognized rules governing such things as size and choice of wood, and drew from a collective heritage the symbols of the heart, cross, cock and fish. But a modern carving of a great anteater on a branch (no. 234)—inspired by a television programme, carved from a piece of driftwood, grooved with an electric drill, and fixed on a base of four toes with red-painted nails—shows a marked freedom from accepted traditions and techniques.

One factor underlying this change in orientation is that the goods needed for basic survival are no longer produced in the home. Furniture and textiles, for example, are now factory-made and produced in volume. Thus, the factory has replaced the workshop, and the machine operator has replaced the craftsman with his homemade tools.

At one time, maple sugar was moulded in forms patiently carved by hand, not only to produce a utilitarian object, but to express the religious or romantic sentiments of the carver; now, maple sap is collected, boiled and packaged mechanically. Butter used to be made by the farmer and brought to market decorated with a hand-carved stamp that he designed himself; today, the butter is prepared in large dairies and sold in standardized bricks. There is little place in the commercial process for artistic flair.

As a consequence, many traditions that established the patterns for certain forms of folk art have become obsolete. The creative urge, carried farther from its traditional sources, finds its expression in innovative ways derived from contemporary influences.

FROM FUNCTION TO FORM

The second tendency, influenced no doubt by the enthusiastic reception of folk art into the art market, indicates that more and more folk art is moving away from functionality toward pure form. Objects of folk art originally had an agreed-upon function in a community, whether it was strictly utilitarian or the expression of a meaningful idea or tradition. The artists worked for their personal satisfaction and that of their immediate group. Now, however, dealers, collectors and museums have contributed to the creation of a folk-art market subject to the laws of all markets—the demand for goods. The pressure of the market carries the folk artist farther and farther toward the expression of purely aesthetic considerations. Many folk artists no longer produce simply for their own satisfaction or for that of their communities. They may orient their works to the tastes of a larger audience, and concentrate on supplying the demand for a particular type of object. Some fall under the influence of dealers and collectors who urge

them to create "to order". Occasionally, "mass production" of similar subjects will occur to satisfy the demand of a clientele hungry for the exotic. The result is what is often called tourist, or airport, art, exemplified by the popular carvings of habitants and other rustic characters in Saint-Jean–Port-Joli, Québec.

Modern technology, especially in the realms of transport and communications, has acquainted us with the farthest reaches of our planet and expanded the dimensions of social groups. Today's folk artists can reach beyond their immediate group to the members of a considerably larger community. Function, whether utilitarian, narrative, or even dramatic, is giving way in much contemporary folk art to an emphasis on form.

FROM COLLECTIVE TO INDIVIDUAL

In the past, folk art was essentially collective, but a pronounced tendency toward individuality has now appeared. Originally, folk artists represented their communities, and their compositions were perceived as witnesses to collective tastes and beliefs. Today, large numbers of folk artists express themselves more as individuals, and their work increasingly reveals personal dimensions. Three pieces that relate the story of Adam and Eve are significant in this regard. A conventional sampler (no. 139) shows rigorous adherence to religious traditions; a later carving illustrating the story (no. 140) shows personal dimensions of candour and a fresh approach to tradition that is at once religious and poetic; the third piece, another carving (no. 141), expresses a disregard for traditional religious interpretation, and proposes an overtly sexual interpretation of original sin. Recent interest by dealers and collectors in non-traditional folk art has no doubt stimulated the creation of works that owe more to personal imagination than to traditional community beliefs. Without totally cutting their roots, many folk artists give free reign to their own fantasies and impulses, sometimes taking a mischievous pleasure in producing something bizarre.

FROM ETHNIC TO UNIVERSAL

Finally, folk art progressively departs from its ethnic origins toward a more universal view. Moved by the physical environment and the cultural characteristics of the community, folk artists of old necessarily borrowed their subjects, techniques and symbols from the traditions of their ethnocultural group. Québec folk artists crowned the steeples of their churches with a weather-cock, the Ukrainians decorated eggs at Easter, the Portuguese sang the fado and the Spaniards danced the flamenco. Today, because of the development of modern communications and the mass immigrations of our era, Canadian folk artists are confronted almost daily with cultural traditions different from their own. These nourish their imaginations and stimulate their creative urges. Thus, a retired suburbanite decorates his garden with exotic animals such as penguins, tigers and giraffes (no. 215), and an isolated farmer conceives an ironic comment on the subject of the Six-Day War between Israel and Egypt (no. 279).

Massive immigration during this century greatly influenced the development of folk art in Canada. While remaining attached to inherited traditions, the immigrant is transformed through contact with the host society. At the same time, society undergoes important modifications as it is confronted with the arrival of a great many foreign traditions. This is as applicable to motifs and symbols in folk art as it is to family relations or social organiza-tion. In concrete terms, if the Irish immigrant willingly exchanges the shamrock for the maple leaf, and the Russian his bear for the beaver, long-settled Canadians might choose to wear a poncho rather than a parka and willingly dance a samba rather than a jig.

These tendencies in folk art certainly do not constitute irreversible movements. They do not necessarily lead to a totally innovative art without any further reference to either the community or ethnocultural group. There are tensions between tradition and innovation, function and form, the collective and the individual, the ethnic and the universal, and all are evidence of broader changes in Canadian society.

Conclusion

Contemporary folk art in Canada has become progressively detached from the traditions that tied it to the utilitarian, and is becoming more directly oriented toward objects that produce aesthetic pleasure. This does not prevent it from being an eminently functional art, a carrier of narrative or dramatic con-tent. Many of its themes, symbols and motifs remain rooted in tradition, although they are expressed with a sense of spontaneity and fantasy. In this way, Canadian folk artists reflect the sensibil-ity of all Canadians, and contribute in their own way to the devel-opment of a national consciousness.

This exhibition celebrates not only the aesthetic appeal of Canadian folk art, but also the honesty and humanity of its cre-ators. Ultimately we are led from objects to the people who create them and then to those who appreciate them. Folk art is indeed a process involving the artists and their communities, not only the communities in which they live, but a wider community that includes us all.

This exhibition offers to Canadians an opportunity to toast their own creative gifts, their own appreciation for beauty, fantasy and humour, and, above all, their own inexhaustible inspiration. Folk artists provide an eloquent interpretation of our deepest aspirations. They express, from the heart, a feeling for life and creativity, for the "benefit and happiness of the people of a young country"[3] who are increasingly aware of their diverse heritage and trust in their singular future.

3   Barbeau, "Les arts traditionnels", p. 57.

Folk Art in Canada

Catalogue Note

TITLES

Until recently, few folk artists titled their works, but, influenced probably by the fine arts and certainly by the demands of the marketplace, contemporary folk artists often give their creations titles. In this exhibition, those given by the artist are shown within quotation marks. Other titles are not, because they are merely descriptive. In a few cases, such as *Clem* (no. 1) or *Ti-Gus* (no. 233), the titles are affectionate nicknames that have come to be associated with the pieces over the course of time. The adoption of nicknames tells folklorists something about people's earlier reactions to a piece.

DIMENSIONS

The sizes are given from the largest to the smallest dimension, and in the case of paintings and wall plaques include the frame.

TRANSLATION

Interviews with folk artists were conducted in either English or French. The French interviews were translated for this edition of the catalogue.

Clem
Uxbridge, Ontario
Twentieth century
Wood, fabric, glass, metal
125 x 40 x 20 cm
CCFCS 77-237

Originally employed as a scarecrow, Clem was retired to a garage in Uxbridge, Ontario, where he was later found. His sturdy personality is the result of an accumulation of small details, from his uncharacteristic lapel button to the tiny ring in his nose. Both arms are articulated, capable of being raised to shoulder height for the traditional scarecrow stance, and a metal handle attached to the base serves for carrying him about. From his blocky feet and the incised muscles on his arms and hands to his expressive jowls and tightly clenched teeth, Clem cuts a figure of workmanlike charm. His realistic appearance must not only have frightened off several generations of crows, but also proved a source of wry amusement for human onlookers.

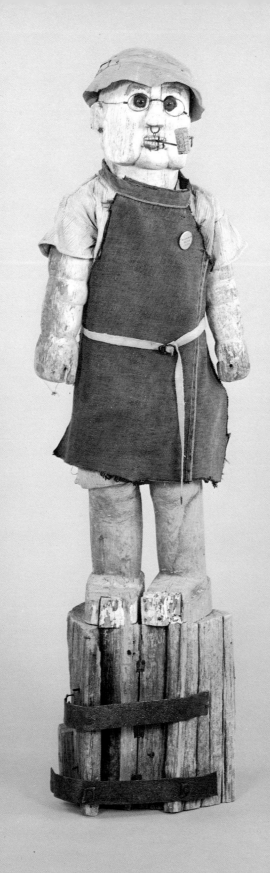

Reflection

The folk art of reflection is a method of recording life, not only the personal experiences of the artists, but recollections of their culture, environment and community.

The basic requirements for survival are food, clothing and shelter, and the tools used to produce them are often among the earliest cultural objects to be shaped and decorated. Hence, this exhibition begins with a collection of tools whose form and ornamentation are based on traditional motifs.

Contemplation of nature and the environment is also an inspiration for certain forms of folk art. In powder horns and weather-vanes, folk artists combined function and beauty, and reflected also on the natural world around them, which was at times an ally, at times an enemy. The challenges of both land and sea are depicted in this category of folk art, as are personal memories, the pain of leaving a cherished land, and the hope that life in the New World will be worth the price of separation.

This new life was to bring yet more change, with modern technology outstripping the methods and traditions developed over centuries and learned over lifetimes. As a result, much of the folk art of reflection records in miniature the skills, amusements and tales of the past, presenting a tangible legacy of community wisdom to the generations to come. If folk art is the echo of life, folk art will inevitably change to suit changing times, and the folk art of reflection will produce new forms and new ideas.

Trivets

(Numbers 2–6)

Trivets were used to support cooking utensils in the fireplace as well as hot objects such as irons. The craftsman often decorated them with various motifs: circles, spirals, tree branches and hearts.

2.
Iron-Holder
Portneuf County, Québec
Nineteenth century
Perforated tin
20.5 x 12.5 x 5 cm
Sharpe Coll., CCFCS 77-1155

3.
Voluted Heart
Cornwall region, Ontario
Nineteenth century
Wrought iron
14 x 12.5 x 3 cm
CCFCS 78-582

4.
Circle
Québec City region, Québec
Nineteenth century
Wrought iron
17 (diam.) x 6 cm
Sharpe Coll., CCFCS 77-1153

5.
Scrolled Heart
Eastern Ontario
Nineteenth century
Wrought iron
14 x 11 x 3.5 cm
Price Coll., CCFCS 79-1605

6.
Pointed Heart
Portneuf County, Québec
Nineteenth century
Wrought iron
17 x 11 x 7.5 cm
Sharpe Coll., CCFCS 77-1154

Roasting Forks

(Numbers 7–9)

Made of wrought iron, these forks were used to handle meat cooking in the fireplace. Their simple ornamentation nevertheless reveals the craftsmen's dexterity and artistic intentions.

7.
Openwork Twist
Pickering, Ontario
Nineteenth century
Wrought iron
39 x 6.5 x 3.5 cm
Price Coll., CCFCS 79-1601

8.
Heart
Havelock, Ontario
Nineteenth century
Wrought iron
44 x 7.5 x 3.5 cm
Price Coll., CCFCS 79-1602

9.
Single Twist
Québec City region, Québec
Nineteenth century
Wrought iron
41 x 4 x 3.5 cm
Sharpe Coll., CCFCS 77-1132

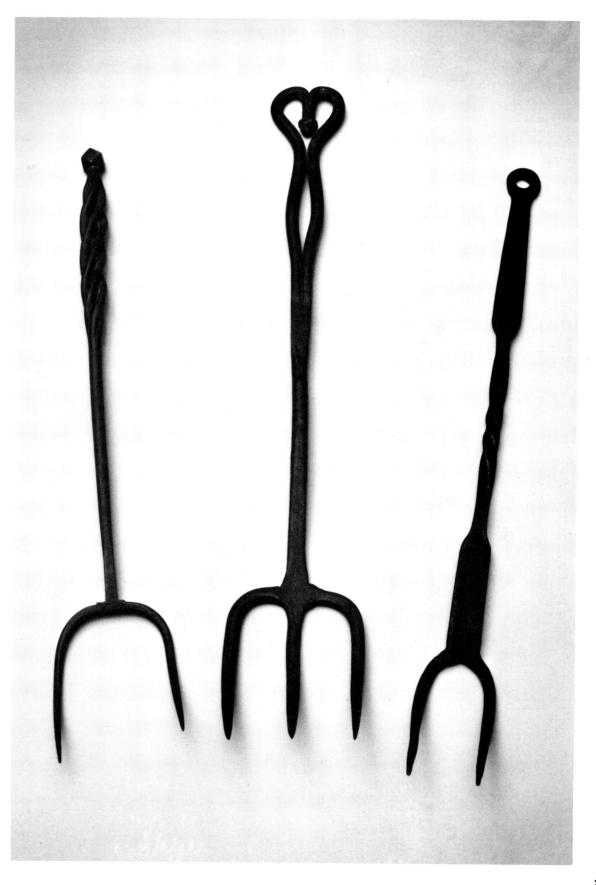

10.
Maple-Syrup Testing Spoon
Québec
Twentieth century
Wood
40.5 x 10 x 5 cm
Sharpe Coll., CCFCS 77-1102

This spoon was used for testing the thickness of maple syrup for eating as taffy. If the little hole below the handle became blocked when the spoon was dipped into the boiling sap, the syrup was ready to be poured over the snow. The craftsman carved this utensil out of a single piece of wood. His artistry is apparent in the ornamentation of the handle.

Crooked Knives

(Numbers 11–16)

Probably of Indian origin, this type of knife cuts when pulled toward the user, unlike the ordinary knife, which is wielded with an outward motion. The handle, bent at an angle of about forty-five degrees, is grasped as one would a pistol, with the fingers pointing upwards and the thumb firmly pressing on the outer curve of the elbow. The blade is made from a used piece of high-quality steel, sometimes from an old file. It is inserted into the handle at a slight angle and twisted upwards slightly so that it is parallel to the cutting surface.

All the knives shown here are from the Maritime Provinces, where they were made in the nineteenth or early twentieth century by the Micmacs or by whites using Indian techniques. The handles are decorated with geometric designs; hearts and diamonds, which are associated with luck, are the most popular motifs. Note, however, that none of the blades has the curved tip characteristic of the original Algonquian tradition.

11.
Crooked Knife
Maritime Provinces
Nineteenth or early twentieth century
Wood, metal
23.5 x 6 x 3 cm
CCFCS 77-714

12.
Crooked Knife
Maritime Provinces
Nineteenth or early twentieth century
Wood, metal
21.5 x 8 x 4 cm
CCFCS 77-716

13.
Crooked Knife
Maritime Provinces
Nineteenth or early twentieth century
Wood, metal
22 x 5.5 x 3.5 cm
CCFCS 77-724

14.
Crooked Knife
Maritime Provinces
Nineteenth or early twentieth century
Wood, metal, string
29 x 7.5 x 4 cm
CCFCS 77-728(a, b)

15.
Crooked Knife
Maritime Provinces
Nineteenth or early twentieth century
Wood, metal
24.5 x 8 x 3.5 cm
CCFCS 77-729(a, b)

16.
Crooked Knife
Maritime Provinces
Nineteenth or early twentieth century
Wood, metal
25 x 7.5 x 5 cm
Price Coll., CCFCS 79-1668

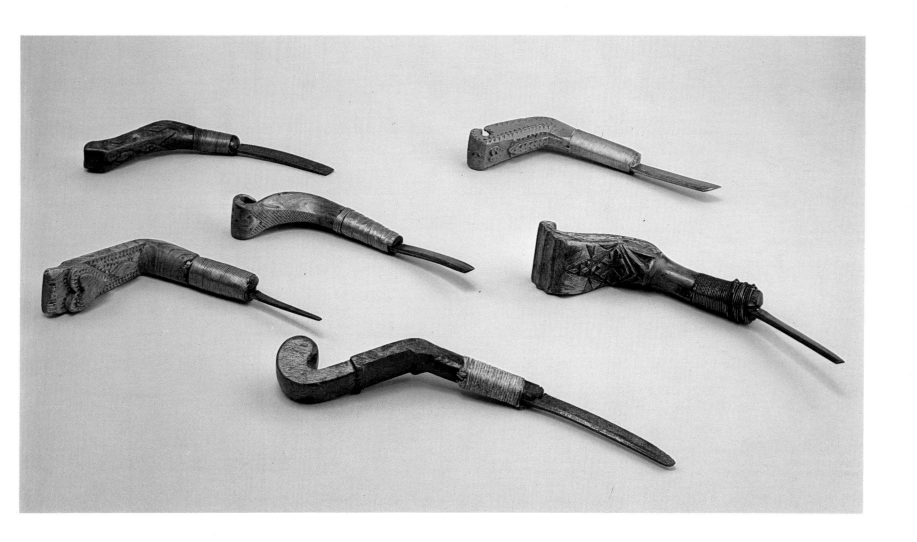

17.
Mallet
Newmarket, Ontario
Late nineteenth century
Wood
39 x 16 x 5.5 cm
Price Coll., CCFCS 79-1670

The gracefully incised design on this basic tool resembles a drawing in pen and ink. The name "Edwin Willis", maker, owner or both, is inscribed on one side, and on the other is displayed on a banner carried by a bird.

18.
Mangle
Alberta
1915
Wood
Mangle: 67 x 9.5 x 4 cm
Roller: 49.5 x 6 (diam.) cm
CCFCS 74-533(1, 2)

Widely known throughout Europe, the
mangle was used to remove water and
wrinkles from freshly washed clothing
and bed-linen. This particular example
was brought to Canada by the
Hutterites. The decoration of a compass-
drawn rosette adds a sprightly touch to
a hard-working tool. It is incised with
the initials "EKH" and the date "1915".

19.
Hackle
Waterloo County, Ontario
Nineteenth century
Wood, wrought iron
64 x 16.5 x 12.5 cm
Price Coll., CCFCS 79-1612

This comb, called a hackle, was used to
dress flax before spinning.

20.
Canoe Cup
Eastern Canada
Early nineteenth century
Wood
12 x 8 x 4.5 cm
Price Coll., CCFCS 79-1671

Voyageurs and hunters travelling by canoe sometimes carried cups carved from the burls of tree trunks. These were profusely decorated with incised motifs, such as a four-leaf clover, a basket of flowers, a beaver, a snake, a mermaid and fish, a boat, or hearts. The small barrel attached to the cup with string serves as a toggle for hanging the cup from the belt. On the outer rim of the work is the inscription, "Antoine Cinqmars"(?).

21.
Butter Paddles
Glengarry County, Ontario
Mid-nineteenth century
Wood
19.5 x 7.5 x 1.5 cm
Price Coll., CCFCS 79-1666(1, 2)

This instrument was used to squeeze out the last of the milk during butter making. Deep horizontal grooves are cut into the inner surface of each paddle, and the flat part of the handle is decorated with a lozenge design. The shape of the paddles is enhanced by the extension of the handle over the blade. Each paddle is carved from a single piece of wood.

Butter Moulds and Stamps

(Numbers 22–28)

Made in the home, butter used to be shaped with moulds, usually cylindrical in shape and fitted with a removable stamp. Sometimes the butter was simply formed into bricks and marked with the producer's seal. The stamps usually displayed geometrical motifs, forage plants, flowers and animals, and sometimes even a stylized family monogram. In addition to serving as a trademark, the stamps were an important indication of the farmer's aesthetic sensibility.

22.
Swan
Origin unknown
Twentieth century
Hardwood
Holder: 12 (diam.) x 10 cm
Stamp: 15 x 8.5 (diam.) cm
CCFCS 72-800

This stamp is engraved with a swan floating on a pond. The border consists of smooth parallel fluting of plain and foliated channels.

23.
Sheep
Origin unknown
Twentieth century
Hardwood
Holder: 9.5 (diam.) x 8.5 cm
Stamp: 12 x 7.5 (diam.) cm
CCFCS 72-798

The sheep on this stamp revels in lush pasture, surrounded by an incised foliated border.

24.
Floral Motif
Québec City region, Québec
Nineteenth century
Hardwood
9 (diam.) x 5.5. cm
Sharpe Coll., CCFCS 77-1241

The plants appear to be the Irish shamrock, the English rose, and the Scotch thistle.

25.
Floral Motif
Québec City region, Québec
Nineteenth century
Softwood
11 (diam.) x 8 cm
Sharpe Coll., CCFCS 77-1245

The stylized floral motif on this stamp is surrounded by a plain border with a serrated edge.

26.
Beaver
Québec City region, Québec
Nineteenth century
Hardwood
11.5 (diam.) x 10 cm
Sharpe Coll., CCFCS 77-1256

This stamp bears two important Canadian symbols, the beaver and the maple leaf, as well as a stylized leafy branch. The edge is decorated with a serrated channel.

27.
Floral Motif
Québec City region, Québec
Nineteenth century
Hardwood
11.5 (diam.) x 9.5 cm
Sharpe Coll., CCFCS 77-1236

The deeply incised floral motif is surrounded by a wide foliated channel and plain inner and outer borders.

28.
Cow
Port Hope, Ontario
Mid-nineteenth century
Hardwood
9 (diam.) x 6 cm
Price Coll., CCFCS 79-1626

This stamp displays a cow under a tree near a fence. The edge is decorated with a finely serrated border.

Powder Horns

(Numbers 29–30)

Before the introduction of cartridges, powder horns were the most common waterproof containers for gunpowder used in muskets, rifles and, later, shotguns. The use of powder horns reached its peak in the eighteenth century, although some horns, such as the large one shown here, may have continued in use well into the nineteenth century. Decorations ranged from traditional scrimshaw designs to deeply incised and coloured geometric figures.

The larger horn bears the name of William Riges, and seems to record an incident at "Wadom" Island (one of the Wadham Islands?) on 16 April 1869, possibly a shipwreck. In addition to assorted sea creatures, several ships are scrimmed onto the surface of the horn, while King Neptune and a traditional mermaid-siren watch over the scene. A rather mysterious figure with a puffin-like nose holds a Union Jack in the centre of the picture.

29.
Powder Horn
Eastern Townships, Québec
Nineteenth century
Animal horn
25.5 x 11 x 7.5 cm
CCFCS 79-362

30.
Powder Horn
Newfoundland
1869
Animal horn
47.5 x 20 x 10 cm
CCFCS 78-418

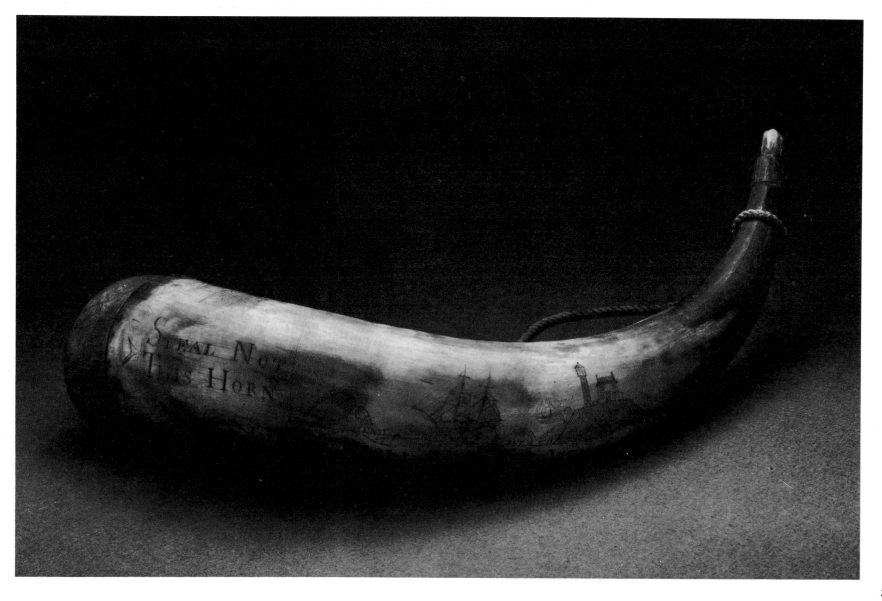

Tobacco Cutters

(Numbers 31–35)

Often made by craftsmen, the tobacco cutter was used until mid-century by smokers who grew their own tobacco. Some of the cutters shown here may have been imported from manufacturers in the United States and Europe; such cutters had a blade support decorated with cut-out or incised motifs, and their popularity encouraged merchants to import them. However, cutters whose wrought-iron motifs were inspired by oral traditions, for example number 35, are much rarer.

31.
Beaver
Saint-Hyacinthe, Québec
Nineteenth or twentieth century
Metal, wood
41 x 19.5 x 17 cm
Sharpe Coll., CCFCS 77-1053

The beaver and the fleur-de-lis near the hinge attest to the use of this piece by French Canadians.

32.
Two Cats and a Fish
Saint-Henri-de-Lévis, Québec
Nineteenth or twentieth century
Metal, wood
35.5 x 19.5 x 16.5 cm
Sharpe Coll., CCFCS 77-1054

33.
Hunting Indian
Lower St. Lawrence region, Québec
Nineteenth or twentieth century
Metal, wood
44 x 20.5 x 20 cm
Sharpe Coll., CCFCS 77-1052

34.
A Celebration of the Horse
Eastern Townships, Québec
Nineteenth or twentieth century
Metal, wood
43 x 20.5 x 18.5 cm
Price Coll., CCFCS 82-136

35.
La Corriveau in a Cage
Saint-Michel-de-Bellechasse, Québec
Nineteenth century
Wrought iron, wood
34 x 20 x 15.5 cm
Sharpe Coll., CCFCS 77-1055

The figurine on the hinge probably
represents La Corriveau in a cage.
Marie-Josephte Corriveau was hanged
in 1763 for killing her husband, and, in
accordance with English practice, her
body was displayed in a cage for several
weeks. This case gave rise to the
Corriveau legend in the nineteenth
century.

Canes

(Numbers 36–40)

The cane is an article cherished by the whittler. It lends itself to a wide variety of decorative motifs, which are sometimes suggested by the natural contours of the branch it was carved from. Coiled serpents and balls in cages are among the most popular motifs. The most ornate canes were undoubtedly the ceremonial ones used on special occasions, such as the Sunday walk.

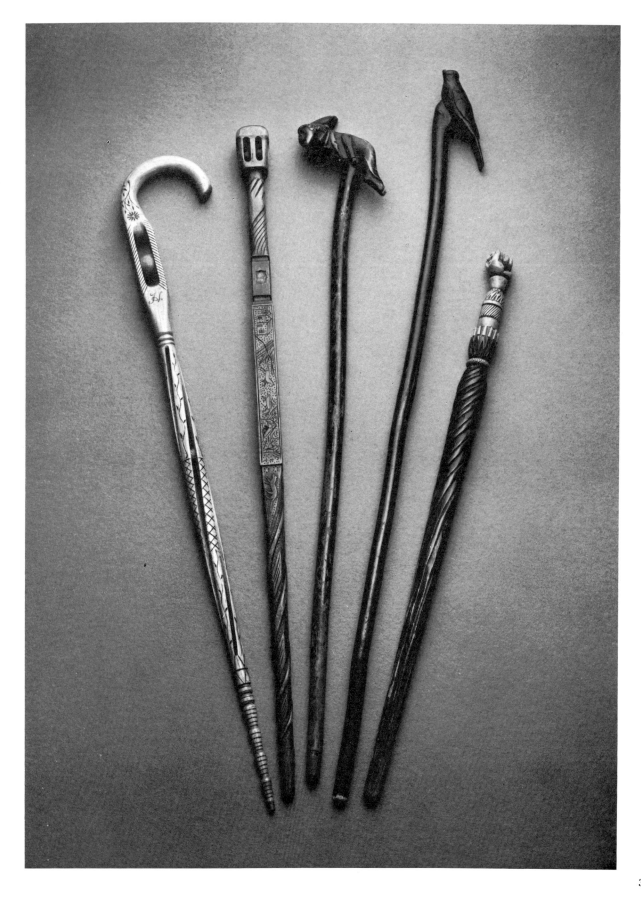

36.
Clearing the Land
Eastern Canada
Nineteenth century
Wood
91 x 4.5 x 4.5 cm
Price Coll., CCFCS 79-1639

This cane is profusely engraved with figurative and symbolic motifs. The four scenes incised on the rectangular section represent events in the life of a typical colonist settling in the Canadian forest—hunting, woodcutting, the finished house set in the first cultivated fields, and the raising of the first animals, represented by poultry. On the lower part of the cane are two snakes, probably symbolizing fertility. A finely incised hand appears just below the pommel, which consists of balls in a cage.

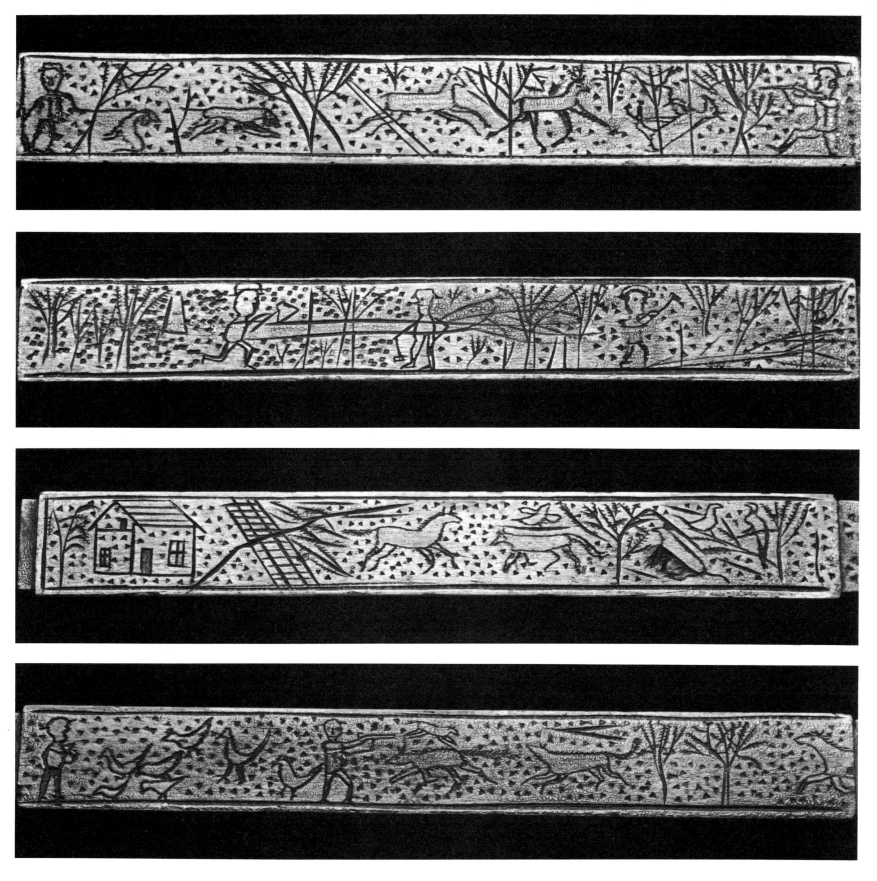

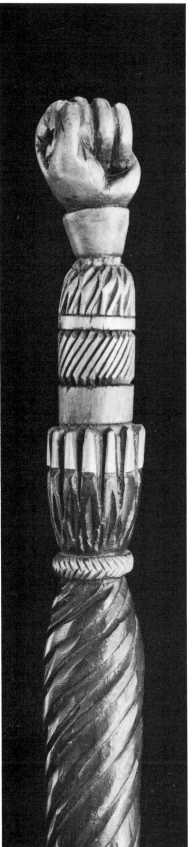

37.
Time in a Cage
Québec
1929
Wood
89.5 x 13.5 x 3.5 cm
CCFCS 80-538

The snakes twining sinuously up the shaft of this cane, as well as the ball in a cage, demonstrate the patience and skill of the sculptor. Decorative plant and geometric motifs fill every available space. Under the cage is the inscription "W M H Sept; 2/1929".

38.
Umbrella
Walt Cooper, Goodwood, Ontario
Twentieth century
Wood
74 x 3.5 (diam.) cm
CCFCS 74-224

This walking stick assumes the form of a furled umbrella, with a pommel in the shape of a closed fist. It evokes the Romantic period in the second half of the nineteenth century, when taking a stroll and contemplating nature was considered a delightful pastime.

39.
Bird
Québec
Twentieth century
Wood
102 x 7.5 x 5 cm
CCFCS 74-218

The bird on the pommel of this cane
was suggested by the shape of the
branch itself.

40.
Elf
Niagara Peninsula, Ontario
Nineteenth century
Wood
93 x 12 x 5.5 cm
CCFCS 78-91

A finely carved elf emerges as though by
magic from a maple branch to form the
pommel of this walking stick, which
displays the imagination and dexterity of
an unknown but very talented artist.

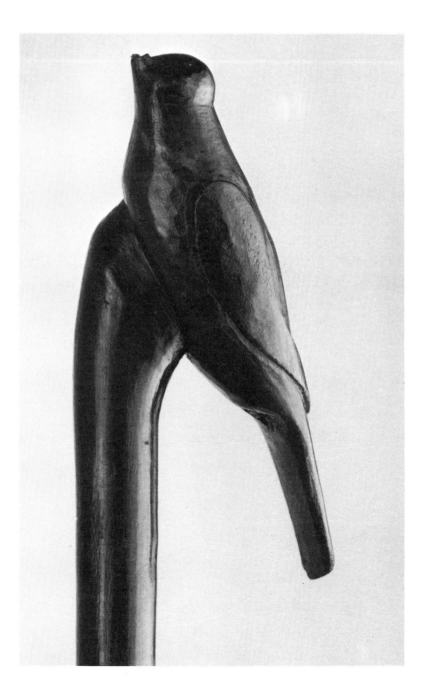

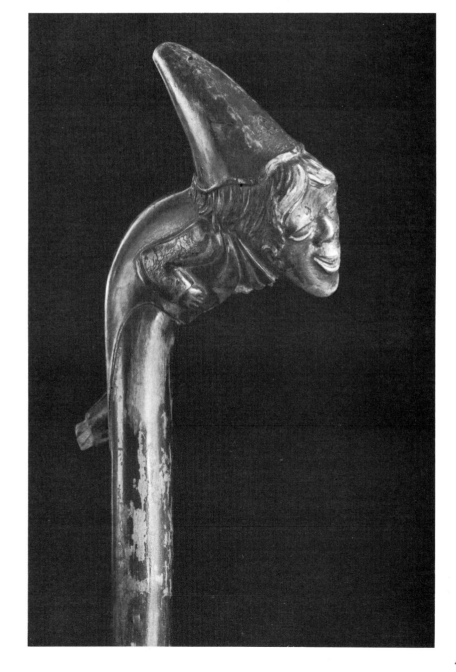

41.
Trinket Box
Captain "Pearly" MacLellan,
Port Greville, Nova Scotia
ca. 1910
Painted wood
42 x 32.5 x 22 cm
CCFCS 77-228

Captain MacLellan made this box for his
daughter Anna Bell while working as
first mate on the ship *Nova Queen*. The
decorative symbols include a ship's
wheel, hearts, and the clasped hands, a
common carver's motif, that appear on
many of Captain MacLellan's other
carvings. The identity of the well-
dressed young man who rides like a
figurehead over the box is not known.

42.
Trinket Box
Cambridge, Ontario
Nineteenth century
Painted tin
24.5 x 20 x 15.5 cm
CCFCS 71-179

This box for letters or other small
personal belongings represents a
tradition probably brought to Southern
Ontario by Pennsylvania Dutch (actually
German) immigrants from the
United States.

43.
Desk Box
Owen Sound, Ontario
Nineteenth century
Wood
51 x 42 x 35.5 cm
CCFCS 74-284

This box was probably used as a lectern and portable desk, and may have held the family Bible. The symbols carved on the front are basically of a religious nature, although the details of their meanings vary from culture to culture. Generally speaking, the sun is a symbol for God, the hens for fruitfulness, and the hearts for love and charity. The fish is an early Christian symbol.

44.
Wall Shelf
Trois-Rivières, Québec
Nineteenth century
Painted wood
78.5 x 32.5 x 20 cm
CCFCS 74-697

Small removable shelves and cabinets were common in nineteenth-century Canadian homes. Fixed to a wall in the kitchen or parlour, they might support a clock or ornament. The shelf-back provided a flat surface ideal for carving or painting.

Wall Cabinets

(Numbers 45–46)

Wall cabinets were common pieces of furniture in nineteenth-century houses, and provided their builders with an opportunity for embellishment. Common design motifs, often applied in profusion, were animals, flowers, hearts and a variety of geometric patterns.

45.
Wall Cabinet
Saint-Ferdinand, Québec
Late nineteenth century
Painted wood, mirror
110 x 43 x 24 cm
Sharpe Coll., CCFCS 77-955

Incised with a complex background, this cabinet is replete with traditional symbols: lovebirds, the tree of life, rosettes, diamonds, fleurs-de-lis, and a harp.

46.
Wall Cabinet
Québec
Early twentieth century
Wood
71 x 46 x 15 cm
CCFCS 78-224

Many pieces of folk art survive without a history, and prompt intrigued speculation. Does this cabinet commemorate a particular boxing match, the boxing careers of two men, or is the fight merely symbolic? And what could be the significance of the three faces above the fighters, juxtaposed with the wooden cross in its neatly carved circular niche?

The rear of the cabinet has been substantially rebuilt, and the recessed area between the boxers probably once contained a mirror.

Chests

(Numbers 47–48)

In Canada, as in Europe, the trunk in its various forms was one of the earliest pieces of furniture, serving not only as a storage box, but also as a bureau or bench. For Canada-bound immigrants, the trunk was the most basic travelling necessity. Its decorations often indicated the owner's origins, status and talent.

47.
Chest
Wilno, Ontario
ca. 1860
Painted wood
110.5 x 68.5 x 54 cm
CCFCS 81-322

An example of the distinctive furniture made in the Polish immigrant communities of Renfrew County, Ontario, this storage chest contains typical Kashubian design elements. Its boards are hand-planed and dovetailed together, and the mouldings are attached by wooden pegs.

48.
Chest
Tracadie, Nova Scotia
Mid-nineteenth century
Painted wood
98 x 48 x 47 cm
CCFCS 79-777

This dower-type six-board chest may have been decorated several years after its construction by, or for, its owner, Mrs. Mary Fougère. All the boards are hand-planed, the nails are hand-forged, and the unplaned bottom shows the marks of an up-and-down saw.

Hooked Rugs

(Numbers 49–52)

Making hooked rugs was part of a system for recovering and making full use of textile fibres in the nineteenth and first half of the twentieth century. Hooking was done on burlap reclaimed from flour and grain sacks. Geometric or naturalistic motifs were drawn on the burlap, which was then stretched over a frame. Generally, scraps of old clothing, yarn made from both new and reclaimed wool, or strands of fibre taken from jute sacks were used. These rugs were laid in special areas of the house, where there was less traffic—in front of armchairs and sofas in the parlour, and beside chests of drawers, desks and beds in bedrooms. It was not until the twentieth century that, under foreign influence, hooked rugs became wall hangings and new fibres were used to make them.

49.
On the Lookout
Québec
Twentieth century
Wool yarn on jute cloth
102 x 63 cm
Sharpe Coll., CCFCS 77-566

Two red deer and an orange bird in a brown tree with multicoloured leaves are on the lookout. A double orange and red floral motif decorates each corner of the rug. These motifs are linked by a double border, also red and orange, which frames the subject.

50.
Leaping Deer
Erin, Ontario
Early twentieth century
Cotton rags and coarse wool yarn
on jute cloth
94 x 90 cm
CCFCS 81-185

A brown deer gambols in a green grove,
surrounded by sprays of red flowers and
green buds, all against a beige
background. The border is of black and
green stripes.

51.
Grey Codfish
Saint-Anselme, Québec
Twentieth century
Wool yarn on jute cloth
93 x 46 cm
Sharpe Coll., CCFCS 77-565

This grey codfish against an ash-grey
background, framed by a double border
of brown and beige, is a typical example
of painstaking hooking done with dyed
reprocessed coarse wool.

52.
Horse
Ruby Tyndell, Palmerston, Ontario
Second quarter of twentieth century
Strips of cotton on jute cloth
99 x 88 cm
CCFCS 81-192

A white horse with a black mane and tail is placed against a black background framed with a herringbone pattern in grey, black and burgundy. The linear hooking is exceptionally uniform, making the rug reversible.

Decoys

(Numbers 53–60)

Early accounts by European settlers mention the awesome numbers of waterfowl in North America and the ingenious use of decoys by the native peoples who hunted them. Settlers quickly adopted the technique of luring game, and the decoy has since become almost a symbol of the outdoor sportsman.

Early decoys were made from a variety of materials, including sticks, straw, skin, canvas and feathers, but, by the turn of the century, decoy makers were producing finely carved and painted wooden forms depicting every detail of particular species. Today, decoys have come to be admired as much for their realism and beauty as for their practical use. Greatly coveted by collectors, decoys made by recognized carvers have found an outlet far removed from either the workshop or the sporting-goods store.

53.
Hooded Merganser
Prescott, Ontario
Mid-twentieth century
Painted wood
28.5 x 15.5 x 13 cm
Price Coll., CCFCS 79-1712

A cocked head with touches of gold paint imparts a lifelike quality to this small decoy.

54.
Canvasback
Charles Morphy,
Carleton Place, Ontario
ca. 1920
Painted wood
42 x 22.5 x 17.5 cm
CCFCS 72-226

Charles Morphy was born in 1875 and worked for Findley's Foundry Limited, in Carleton Place, Ontario. After he left the foundry he worked for a local sporting-goods store. He was a well-known hunter in the area and a self-taught carver.

55.
Black-bellied Plovers
Prince Edward Island
Late nineteenth century
Painted wood
47.5 x 27.5 x 23.5 cm
Price Coll., CCFCS 79-1717; 79-1718

This type of decoy is referred to as a "stick-up" because it is planted in the sand along a beach to attract shorebirds.

56.
Canada Goose
George and James Warin,
Toronto, Ontario
ca. 1870
Painted wood
60 x 24.5 x 23 cm
Price Coll., CCFCS 79-1690

George and James Warin were
boatbuilders who emigrated from
England to Toronto in the mid-1800s.
As well as making boats, both brothers
carved and hunted ducks and geese. In
1894, George was one of the founding
members of the St. Clair Flats Shooting
Company on Lake St. Clair, Ontario.

57.
Black Duck
The Burleigh brothers, Toronto, Ontario
ca. 1900
Painted wood
42.3 x 16.7 x 16.4 cm
CCFCS 80-174

There were four Burleigh brothers
—Edward, Clarence, Norman and
George—all from the Ashbridges Bay
area of Toronto. They were "market
gunners", making their living in the
autumn by hunting wildfowl.

58.
Green-winged Teal
Henry Townson,
Fisherman Island, Toronto Harbour,
Lake Ontario
ca. 1920
Painted wood
31 x 13.5 x 13 cm
CCFCS 80-389

Henry Townson is known to have carved
very few birds, all of them in the early
1920s. An avid sportsman, he was a
member of the Toronto Gun Club.

59.
Guzzler
Angus Lake, West Lake, Ontario
Early twentieth century
Painted wood
52 x 15.5 x 11 cm
Price Coll., CCFCS 79-1695

Angus Lake, the postmaster of West Lake, in Prince Edward County, was a prolific decoy carver in the 1920s and 1930s. Some of his decoys are signed simply "A".

This decoy is referred to as a "guzzler" because of its posture, which suggests to passing flocks that it is feeding or possibly driving away a rival, thus indicating that all is safe on the water below.

60.
Common Goldeneye
Sam Hutchings, Elgin, Ontario
ca. 1920
Painted wood
29.5 x 14.5 x 10.5 cm
CCFCS 80-176

Sam Hutchings was born in 1894, and worked as a trapper, truck driver and farmer. He started hunting and carving in about 1910, making his decoys at an average rate of four a day from cedar fence-posts or pine.

61.
Rooster
Collins Eisenhauer,
Union Square, Nova Scotia
ca. 1975
Painted wood and metal
44 x 37 x 13.5 cm
CCFCS 77-385

Three-dimensional portraiture of
animals is a traditional pursuit of
carvers. Collins Eisenhauer, known for
his life-sized figures and humorous
miniatures, also carved a series of birds
and other animals with which to
decorate his front yard. Compared with
his later work, the calico-patterned
rooster is almost plain, but in paying
just the right attention to detail, as in the
cockscomb and tail, Mr. Eisenhauer has
created a memorable image of the king
of the barnyard.

62.
Cat
Belleville, Ontario
Early twentieth century
Painted wood
58.5 x 30 x 10 cm
CCFCS 79-1726

The weathered texture of this carving indicates that it probably stood outdoors. The weathering also reveals a lamination technique so complex as to be a veritable puzzle. This is probably the result of the creator of the piece having access to only relatively thin pieces of wood. The carving may be a portrait of the family pet.

63.

Cow
Marguerite Mougeot-Raby,
Thurso, Québec
1967
Painted plywood
244 x 181 x 4.5 cm
CCFCS 80-678

A dynamic woman in her thirties, Marguerite Mougeot-Raby lives with her husband and four children on a farm on the north shore of the Ottawa River. Although she shares the various farm tasks with her husband, she spends her leisure time decorating the barn and the sheepfold. These *garnitures* (trimmings), as she calls them, are usually paintings of domestic animals. The artist applies house paint in bright colours on large panels of plywood attached to the gable ends of the barn and the sheepfold. Facing this cow on the north gable of the barn was a bull of the same size. On the south gable is a painting of a calf. The sheep that decorates the sheepfold was exhibited at the Papineauville agricultural fair in 1980 to publicize sheep-raising in the region. Mrs. Mougeot-Raby has proved that daily life can be a source of inspiration for those who have inherited from their elders a certain aesthetic sense along with dexterity.

64.
Ox-Head
New Brunswick
Early twentieth century
Painted wood, animal horn
80 x 68 x 43 cm
CCFCS 77-314

This ox-head carving originally came
from New Brunswick, but was found
hanging on a farmer's fence in Port
Maitland, Nova Scotia. The finely
modelled head is carved from a single
piece of wood except for the ears and, of
course, the horns, which may have been
taken from one of the beasts it
memorializes.

65.
Great Blue Heron
Billy Andrews, Bradford, Ontario
1977
Painted wood
166 x 121 x 28 cm
CCFCS 78-184

Billy Andrews was an English orphan
who came to Canada in the 1920s. He
became the hired hand on a Bradford
farm and never left. Explaining his
motivation for carving, he said, "When I
first came here, I hadn't much to do; I
thought, well, gol', I'm gonna start
carving, whittlin' as they called it." Mr.
Andrews combined carving and farm
work for many years, producing a great
many figures, including birds, farm
animals, and scenes from his youth.
The *Great Blue Heron* combines
carving, painting, and the delicate
addition of individually made wooden
feathers. "If anyone can get my carving
and get enjoyment out of it," the artist
said, "that's great."

66.
Seagull and Fish
Ralph Boutilier,
Milton, Queens County, Nova Scotia
1975
Painted wood and tin
170 (with stand) x 70 x 61 cm
CCFCS 77-370

As a young man Ralph Boutilier worked
for his father, who was a tugboat
captain. He went to sea himself, but also
accumulated a handyman's collection of
skills. His experience with painting,
carpentry and mechanics is evident in
his most ambitious and best-known
creations, whirligigs of flying birds.
Already skilled in model shipbuilding
and in painting for tourists,
Mr. Boutilier in 1968 turned to making
"something beautiful to go with the
wind". Despite a few false starts,
experiments over the years have yielded
a flock of wind-driven birds: a Blue Jay,
kingfisher, two eagles and this gull.

67.
Codfish
Randall Smith, Ingomar, Nova Scotia
ca. 1975
Painted wood, metal
104 x 29.5 x 14.5 cm
CCFCS 80-90

Born in 1906, Randall Smith has lived all his life on the Atlantic coast, working as a fisherman, boatbuilder and carpenter. He has always done some carving in his spare time, using the same tools he makes his living with. His favourite subjects are fish, which he says, "I know all about." This codfish was made to stand on a pole in the yard. Currently, Mr. Smith is carving sharks about 1.5 metres long.

68.
Prize Horse
S.C. Butler, Aylmer, Ontario
ca. 1890
Paint on hardboard
91.5 x 60.5 cm
CCFCS 78-208

The usual subjects for the itinerant artist were family portraits, but farmers also often requested pictorial records of proud possessions—their homes, cattle and horses. Today this tradition survives in a somewhat altered form in paintings on the sides of barns; these usually represent the breed raised on a particular farm rather than an individual animal.

69.
"Seagulls"
Joseph Norris,
Lower Prospect, Nova Scotia
1974
Enamel on plywood
63.5 x 63.5 x 2 cm
CCFCS 77-391

Joe Norris had to quit his career as a fisherman when he was struck by a heart attack at the age of forty-nine. He began painting while he was convalescing and has been at it ever since, sometimes up to twelve hours a day. He works without preparatory sketches or drawings, but has a good idea of what he wants to do when he starts. His favourite subjects are the waterfront, the sea and fishing. Mr. Norris is a bachelor but never wants for company. Neighbours, children and customers stream in and out of his little house in Lower Prospect to have a chat and watch him work. In this painting he has set the fisherman's omnipresent companion, the seagull, against a familiar background of hills and sea.

Weather-Vanes

(Numbers 70–76)

The custom of erecting weather-vanes on buildings no doubt originated in the ancient rites associated with the completion of a structure. That same tradition is the source of not only the original roof-peak decorations, which symbolize a job completed and appeal for the protection of kindly spirits, but also the personalized weather-vane signs of Europe, brief dramas in the sky depicting the daily acts of craftsmen and labourers. In addition to acting as a weather gauge and informing the passer-by of the inhabitant's occupation, the weather-vane displays its creator's technical dexterity and aesthetic sensibility. The most common motifs on Canadian weather-vanes are the horse, the cow, the beaver, the fish, and especially the cock.

In its effort to Christianize established customs, the Church began in the ninth century to crown its places of worship with the rooster, which in Egyptian and Greek mythology symbolized resurrection and vigilance, two themes of Christian teaching since its beginnings. The custom of putting cocks on church belfries has been especially common in Québec, and was extended to wayside crosses. These roosters are evidence of Québec's French and Christian heritage.

70.
Trotting Horse
Iroquois region, Ontario
Late nineteenth century
Reinforced tin
132.5 x 120 x 38 cm (with support)
Price Coll., CCFCS 79-1590

This spirited horse displays the craftsman's artistry.

71.
Beaver Eating a Maple Leaf
L'Assomption, Québec
Twentieth century
Soldered tin
72 x 29 x 6.5 cm
Sharpe Coll., CCFCS 77-1045

Its fine detail makes this weather-vane a true work of art, incorporating the two most common Canadian symbols.

72.
Trout
A. Durangeau, La Prairie, Québec
Twentieth century
Painted soldered tin
68 x 30.5 x 30 cm (with support)
Sharpe Coll., CCFCS 77-945

This painted tin trout with glass eyes,
mounted on a tin ventilation cap,
pointed out the wind direction as an
arrow would.

73.
Cock
Louiseville, Québec
Early nineteenth century
Painted tar-covered metal
95 x 85 x 36 cm (with support)
Price Coll., CCFCS 79-1587

This powerful bird and a colleague
probably watched over the destiny of
the old twin-steepled church in
Louiseville, which was built in 1804 and
demolished a century later, in 1917.

74.
Cock
Québec
Mid-nineteenth century
Soldered metal
107 x 71 x 35 cm (with support)
Price Coll., CCFCS 79-1588

The rounded and stylized contours of
this rooster reveal an impression, not
without humour, of pent-up force.

75.
Cock
Saint-Adelphe, Québec
Nineteenth century
Painted soldered tin
82 x 57 x 23 cm (with support)
CCFCS 77-503

76.
Cock
Sainte-Blandine, Québec
Nineteenth century
Painted softwood, tin
70 x 59 x 21 cm
CCFCS 71-309

A venerable patriarch having suffered the ravages of time, this rooster, totally Gallic in appearance, recalls the French origins of the Québec people.

77.
"Gem of the Forest"
Stanley Williamson, Gananoque, Ontario
Early twentieth century
Painted wood and plaster
226.5 x 152 x 12.5 cm
CCFCS 75-1162

"Gem of the Forest" must have been a popular sight at the Southern Ontario fairs where Stanley Williamson showed it, along with his other paintings and carvings. A prolific carver and painter since childhood of "all kinds of things", as his sister puts it, Mr. Williamson became a well-known tombstone carver and sign-painter in southeastern Ontario.

Combining his talents in *"Gem of the Forest"*, the artist portrays a romanticized, yet vibrant, view of a natural environment often dreamt about but rarely experienced by Canadians—that of virgin forest, clear streams, and quiet Indian campsites.

GEM OF THE FOREST

78.
Canoeing Scene
Mr. Gandier, Lindsay, Ontario
1920
Painted wood
54 x 35 x 3 cm
Price Coll., CCFCS 79-1659

This low-relief carving is somewhat unusual in that its overall effect is attained by the contrast of painted with plain wood. Only the Indian and the fauna are coloured, thereby creating the subtle illusion of low-lying mist.

79.
"Nekola Kowalski House"
Ann Harbuz,
North Battleford, Saskatchewan
1979
Oil on canvas
102 x 71 x 2.5 cm
CCFCS 79-596

Ann Harbuz is a painter who tells stories, recording on canvas images of the early years of her life in rural Saskatchewan. In her painting of the house of Nekola Kowalski, the village blacksmith, minute details give the work a narrative quality. Although many of Mrs. Harbuz's pictures refer in some way to her Ukrainian heritage, she captures elements of the experience of all Prairie pioneers.

80.
"Bannockburn Outbuildings"
 J. Bruce, Ontario
1889
Oil on canvas
70.5 x 51 x 3 cm
CCFCS 77-479

Bannockburn lies between Brucefield
and Varna in Ontario's Huron County. It
was designated as a post office in 1862.
In this painting, the stone and wooden
buildings are reminiscent of architectural
types well known in Scotland.

81.
Home
Eastern Townships, Québec
Late nineteenth century
Oil on wood
84.5 x 35 x 9 cm
CCFCS 77-461

This stark, precisely composed painting on a single wide board originated in the Eastern Townships of Québec.

82.
"The Schooner 'Fairy'"
Nova Scotia
Late nineteenth century
Paint on wood
36.5 x 36.5 x 2 cm
CCFCS 76-464

This painting portrays the schooner *Fairy*, out of Shelburne, Nova Scotia. It employs a traditional maritime motif—a ship leaving a shoreline that is marked by a lighthouse. On the back of the pine board are written in pencil the enigmatic words, "20 day of June took the cow away."

83.
"Prairie Home"
Harvey McInnes,
Zealandia, Saskatchewan
1978
Pencil on paper
61 x 49.5 x 2.5 cm
CCFCS 79-493

For Harvey McInnes, a boyhood interest
in drawing developed into an important
means of expression in adult life,
especially after he sold his farm and
retired. Although his pictures generally
portray life on the Prairie farm, the
specific subject of any drawing takes
second place to a mood of
contemplation, serenity and stillness.
Working exclusively with coloured
pencils, the artist achieved the warm
evening glow in this picture by starting
with a yellow background and then
building his composition, bit by bit,
until it seemed to him just right.

84.
"Fall Sunset"
Wesley Dennis, Brownlee, Saskatchewan
1967
Oil on canvas
81 x 58.5 x 5.5 cm
CCFCS 79-566

Wesley Dennis, a retired farmer, was a
meticulous recorder of the history and
natural life of the Prairies. A self-taught
artist, he began by copying
reproductions, and then, with his wife
Eva, who also took up painting after
their marriage, he began to paint his
memories.

"Fall Sunset" depicts the town of
Archive, Saskatchewan, before the Co-op
elevator was torn down. "An elevator
has a presence," Mr. Dennis said, "and
if you don't feel that presence, you are
wasting your time trying to paint one."

85.
"Barr Colony, First Settlers in Saskatoon, 1903"
C. N. Frey,
North Vancouver, British Columbia
1910–20
Oil on canvas
183.5 x 92.5 x 2.5 cm
Price Coll., CCFCS 77-406

C. N. Frey lived much of his later life in British Columbia as a landscape gardener and proprietor of the C. N. Frey Scenic Company, but his interest in painting can be traced back to his youth in Ontario. Moving to Calgary in 1908, he advertised his services as a "General Illustrator and Topographical Real Estate Artist". That might explain the merging of landscape painting and map-making in this picture, with its labels and compass directions, which was painted after his move to Calgary.

The Barr Colony grew out of the Reverend I. M. Barr's recruitment of British colonists, who settled a town on the Saskatchewan–Alberta border that is still known as Lloydminster after the colonists' chaplain, George Exton Lloyd.

In 1920, Mr. Frey moved to British Columbia, a move that coincided with his growing interst in what he called "cosmic science", which changed the character of his later works.

86.
"Souvenir de l'heureuse famille François Mailhot"
(Memento of the Happy François Mailhot Family)
Québec
1896
Oil on canvas
119 x 81.5 x 3 cm
Price Coll., CCFCS 79-1652

This panorama of a period is notable for its lively illustration of the elements of traditional life, from the buildings and various activities to the people of the time. Note the fisherman, the boatmen, and the priest talking with the landowner, the notary with the craftsman and the nun with the lady of the house. Note also the bread oven and the potash kettle set back from the house.

87.
"Wreck of the 'Torhamvan', Ferryland"
Arch Williams,
Ferryland, Newfoundland
1977
Oil on canvas
71.5 x 56.5 x 2 cm
CCFCS 78-122

Arch Williams, fisherman and store clerk, was born in 1909 on the southern shore of Newfoundland and has lived there ever since. He began painting in school and it became an ongoing hobby, a means of recording the history of his coastal home. A mid-seventies radio interview led to an increased measure of recognition and to the subsequent sale of his paintings in the Maritimes and beyond.

88.
"Exhaustion II"
Cornelius Van Ieperen,
Consul, Saskatchewan
1978
Oil on hardboard
48.5 x 38.5 x 4.5 cm
CCFCS 79-780

Although Cornelius Van Ieperen was a very young boy when he arrived on the Prairies in 1912, he vividly remembers the struggles of those early years and his growing awareness of the dramatic beauty of the open country. In later life, when multiple sclerosis confined him to a wheelchair, he forced himself to try to paint his impressions and memories. With the encouragement of his wife and friends, Mr. Van Ieperen has developed skill in a variety of techniques. This painting is among his favourites: "A terribly cold day with the sun shining and a sun on each side called sun-dogs! You couldn't stand the wind. You had lots of snow. Well, you played out and the horse played out and you better find shelter."

89.
Sawyers' Whirligig
Western Ontario
Early twentieth century
Painted wood, metal
59 x 45 x 40 cm
CCFCS 75-906

In common use in the St. Lawrence
Valley in the seventeenth century, pit
saws were an efficient method of sawing
planks from a large log. Early sawyers
were itinerant, travelling from pit to pit
with their own tools. This outdoor
ornament, a stylized representation of
an early saw-pit, at one time had a vane
that turned it into the wind for effective
movement of the propeller, the saw and
the three figures. The building exhibits
extensive chip-carving.

90.
"The Limbs Are Tough"
Bernie Wren, Langley, British Columbia
Late 1970s
Painted wood
120 x 46.5 x 4 cm
CCFCS 79-368

The lumberjack topping a tree is a
common theme in the work of Bernie
Wren, who as a young man worked as a
topper and carpenter in British
Columbia logging camps. After retiring
in 1975, Mr. Wren had time to do what
he wished. Dissatisfied with his initial
attempts at painting, he began to carve,
and was delighted at the enthusiastic
response to his work. He has found that
his carved and brightly coloured scenes
of logging and of the aspects of West
Coast life he knows best are the most
popular. Carving for Bernie Wren has
become a bridge between the working
past and a fulfilling life in the present.

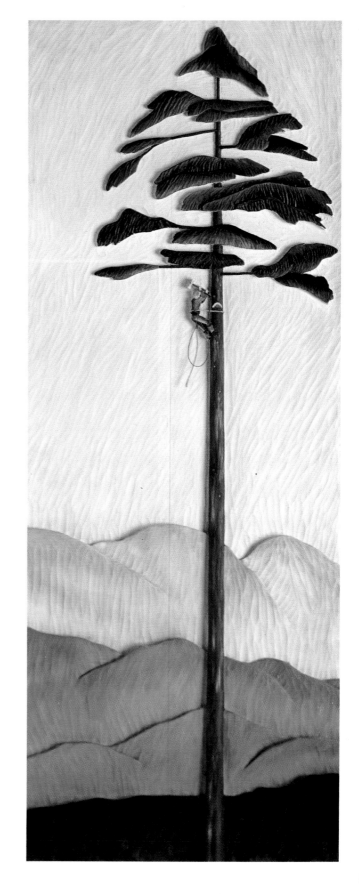

91.
Stump Pulling
René Lavoie, Château-Richer, Québec
Early twentieth century
Painted wood
89 x 27.5 x 24 cm
Price Coll., CCFCS 79-1727

The Québec woodcarving tradition dates as far back as the mid-eighteenth century, and carving remains important today. Much of the early work was subsidized by the Church, and particular families and regions became well known over the generations for their skill. Two distinct branches of the carving tradition developed, one specializing in holy images, altarpieces and other church decorations; the second depicted working men, such as the habitant or voyageur, but this tradition became romanticized and mass-produced to the point of cliché. This model portraying the clearing of land maintains the vigour for which Québec carvers are noted.

92.
Pig Butchering
Fred Moulding, Regina, Saskatchewan
ca. 1970
Painted wood, tin
28 x 20 x 11.5 cm
CCFCS 79-581

Around 1960 Fred Moulding began to
make models of the tools and farm
equipment that had been so much a
part of his early working life. The
Prairie farmer's excellent memory for
detail enabled him to recreate in
miniature the activities and settings of
the various kinds of work essential to
the farming community. Mr. Moulding
created the hog-butchering scene "to
show the young people what life was
like".

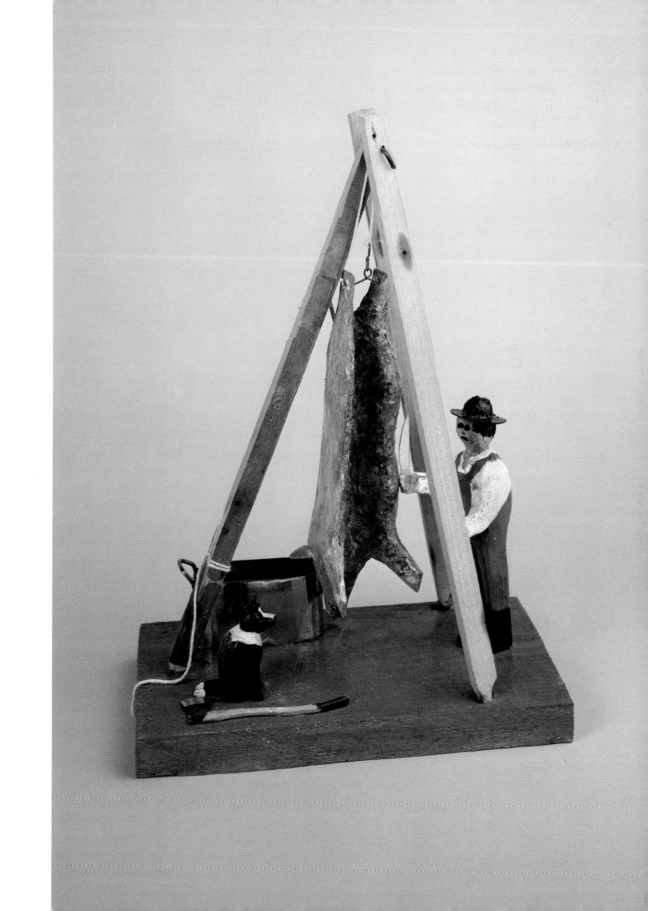

Women's Farm Work

(Numbers 93–97)

Fred Moulding's miniatures document his memories of early Prairie farm life. He takes his work to local fairs and exhibitions, and although he is well known as a maker of miniature wagons and horse-drawn vehicles, his conversations with women visitors have led him to represent their role more fully in his models. This group of miniatures records five well-remembered farm chores traditionally performed by women.

93.
Pea-Podding
Fred Moulding, Regina, Saskatchewan
Late 1970s
Painted wood, tin
12.5 x 11.5 x 10 cm
CCFCS 79-574

94.
Butter Churning
Fred Moulding, Regina, Saskatchewan
Late 1970s
Painted wood
11.5 x 10 x 6 cm
CCFCS 79-583

95.
Washing
Fred Moulding, Regina, Saskatchewan
Late 1970s
Painted wood, tin
11.5 x 10.5 x 9.5 cm
CCFCS 79-586

96.
Breadmaking
Fred Moulding, Regina, Saskatchewan
Late 1970s
Painted wood, tin
13 x 12.5 x 11.5 cm
CCFCS 79-575

97.
Pumping Water
Fred Moulding, Regina, Saskatchewan
Late 1970s
Painted wood, tin
12.5 x 12.5 x 7.5 cm
CCFCS 79-582

93

94

95

96

97

89

98.
Logging Camp
Alfred Morneault,
Edmundston, New Brunswick
1978
Natural and painted wood
244 x 73 x 47 cm
CCFCS 80-2

After making extensive notes on his memories of the past, Alfred Morneault said to himself one day, "I can build all that." This was the beginning of a long series of works, recreating in three dimensions, for future generations, the deeds and actions of Madawaska's ancestors. "It is a mission that I have to undertake," he has said, "to teach upcoming generations about the way of life of their ancestors." His objectives were summed up in this sign, placed in full view in his basement workroom: "I am not a sculptor. I work with wood.

I am a whittler. God is my witness to all the truth that I put into my work. 21 June 1977, at seventy-five years of age [translation]."

Alfred Morneault is a man of the woods. Even today he cuts his own wood. His memories of the forester's life are still particularly vivid. This scene represents the construction of a camp at the beginning of a felling period that could last three or four years. Twenty-eight persons are busily working on various jobs. The hunter, the cook and his helpers, the carpenters, everyone is contributing in his own way to the construction of the most comfortable camp possible. The building on the left was to house the dormitory, the one on the right the dining hall and the kitchen. The canvas tent was used as a temporary shelter during construction.

99.
Plowing with Oxen
William Stefanchuk, Tolstoi, Manitoba
Mid-twentieth century
Painted wood and plaster, metal, fabric
82 x 30 x 21 cm
CCFCS 75-2

William Stefanchuk immigrated in the mid-1930s and began farming on the Prairies. He had been a carriage maker in the Ukraine, and in Canada he continued to make carts and carriages, but in miniature. In this creation, the man behind the plow represents the carver himself.

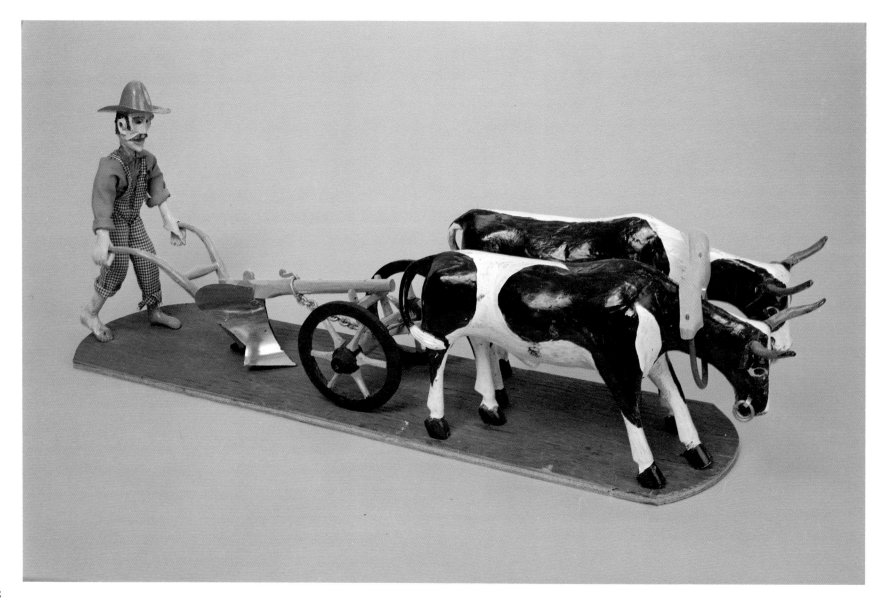

100.
Stoneboat
Octave Verret,
Edmundston, New Brunswick
Mid-twentieth century
Painted wood, leather, plastic,
metal, cotton
78 x 33 x 16 cm
CCFCS 74-1339

In his mid-forties, Octave Verret experienced medical problems that left him an invalid. To pass the time he began to carve scale models of horses pulling traditional wagons and farm implements, things that were close to his heart and clear in his memory. As a younger man, he had been a shingle-cutter, a farmer and a shoemaker, and he carried over his skills in working with wood and leather into this new endeavour. Mr. Verret's models illustrate details of his past life; for example, the male figures all appear with pipes in their mouths because "everyone smoked pipes in those days."

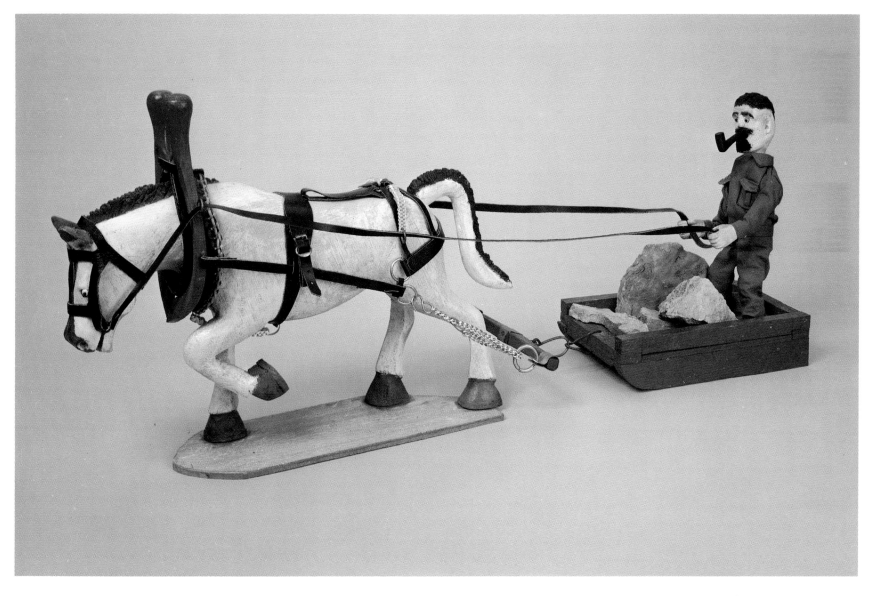

Wagons and Sleighs

(Numbers 101–102)

As a young boy at the turn of the century, Erskine Brown was familiar with the various farm wagons and machines pulled by horses and oxen. Years later, retired and living alone, Mr. Brown turned to reproducing those vehicles of the past in carved wooden models. The *Pioneer Wagon* represents the artist's effort to describe visually the harsh life of the early settlers, while the *Sleigh Ride* captures a tradition from his own experience.

101.
Pioneer Wagon
Erskine Brown, Thornbury, Ontario
1961–74
Painted wood, metal
82 x 40 x 39 cm
CCFCS 74-1012

102.
Sleigh Ride
Erskine Brown, Thornbury, Ontario
1961–74
Painted wood, leather, metal
67 x 27 x 22.5 cm
CCFCS 74-1014

103.
"Pacifique canadien 2400"
(The Canadian Pacific 2400)
Léon Ipperciel, Montebello, Québec
ca. 1965
Painted plywood, metal
240 x 60 x 37 cm
CCFCS 81-158

This scale model was done from memory and is part of a series tracing the history of the steam locomotive from 1829 to 1929. The artist worked on the railroad when he was seventeen and eighteen years of age. "I would have liked to be an engineer, but they wouldn't let me. I was told that it would be too hard for me." Yet, when he became a farmer, the hard work did not prevent him from successfully raising a family and being active in municipal politics for twenty-five years. At the age of sixty-five, he retired: "One fine day, someone came and bought my land." He acquired a house in the village: "Here, one settles in and putters." He was finally able to make his lifelong dream come true, to control the magic of steam. He built thirteen scale models of locomotives that move on rails just as real engines do.

104.
Fishermen
Gaspé region, Québec
Early twentieth century
Painted wood
38 x 17.5 x 11 cm
CCFCS 77-733

This carving of fishermen with their catch piled around them was acquired in the Gaspé region. Two of the fish have nails partly driven into their mouths, with a fragment of twine attached, indicating that they may once have hung outside the boat. Perhaps originally a toy, the harsh simplicity of the carving and the stark colours capture a deep feeling for the fisherman's life.

105.
Half-Model Schooner
Mahone Bay, Nova Scotia
ca. 1900
Painted wood, thread, fabric
92 x 71 x 11 cm
G. Ferguson Coll., CCFCS 81-81

This fully-rigged half-model is known to have hung over the fireplace of a cottage in Mahone Bay, Nova Scotia, in the 1920s. It dates from the period when shipping and shipbuilding brought prosperity to the local economy. Shipowners and crew members often had their favourite craft represented in paintings, half-models or shadow boxes, which they hung in a prominent place in their homes for all to see.

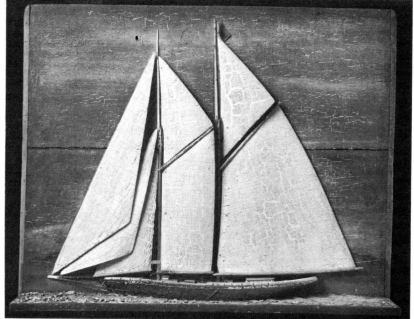

Boat Models

(Numbers 106–107)

Stanley Williamson was born in
Gananoque, Ontario, in the 1870s,
when his hometown was a bustling port
on the St. Lawrence. He became a stone
carver and sign painter, but always
found the time to carve and paint
miniatures, often of the boats that
worked the river. For over twenty years
these were sold at the hardware store in
Gananoque. The speedboat is a faithful
reproduction of a local excursion craft
that plied the waters of the Thousand
Islands. The *"Corsecan"* is a model of a
much larger cruise ship, but is built
with a similar combination of boldness
and attention to detail.

106.
"Corsecan"
Stanley Williamson, Gananoque, Ontario
Early twentieth century
Painted wood, metal and string
91 x 64 x 25 cm
CCFCS 77-8

107.
Speedboat Ride
Stanley Williamson, Gananoque, Ontario
Early twentieth century
Painted wood, metal, fabric
99 x 23 x 20 cm
CCFCS 73-62

Toy Horses

(Numbers 108–110)

There are various types of traditional toy horses known in Canada and throughout the world. Possibly beginning with the stick-horse—a simple block of wood attached to a branch placed between the rider's legs—toy horses developed in many forms, such as the rocking-horse, the pull-toy, and the "shoofly", a seat suspended between flat profiles of a galloping horse. Beyond their role as children's playthings, they stand on their own merits as carvings.

108.
Rocking-Horse
Berthier region, Québec
Nineteenth century
Painted wood, horsehair
76 x 51 x 34 cm
CCFCS 70-116

109.
Rocking-Horse
Rosaire Leblanc,
Sainte-Sophie-de-Lévrard, Québec
Mid-twentieth century
Painted wood, leather, horsehair
65.5 x 52 x 25 cm
Sharpe Coll., CCFCS 77-887

110.
Horse and Cart Pull-Toy
Québec City region, Québec
Nineteenth century
Painted wood, leather, horsehair
71 x 32 x 28 cm
CCFCS 77-229(1, 2)

111.
The Dance Party
René Lavoie, Château-Richer, Québec
Early twentieth century
Painted wood
93.5 x 48.5 x 30 cm
Price Coll., CCFCS 79-1728

The shadow box, or miniature scene in an enclosed setting, has been a popular form of folk expression in many parts of Canada. In Québec, where the wood-carving tradition has a long history, artists like René Lavoie specialized in depicting various aspects of daily life, including people at work or enjoying one another's company on a special evening.

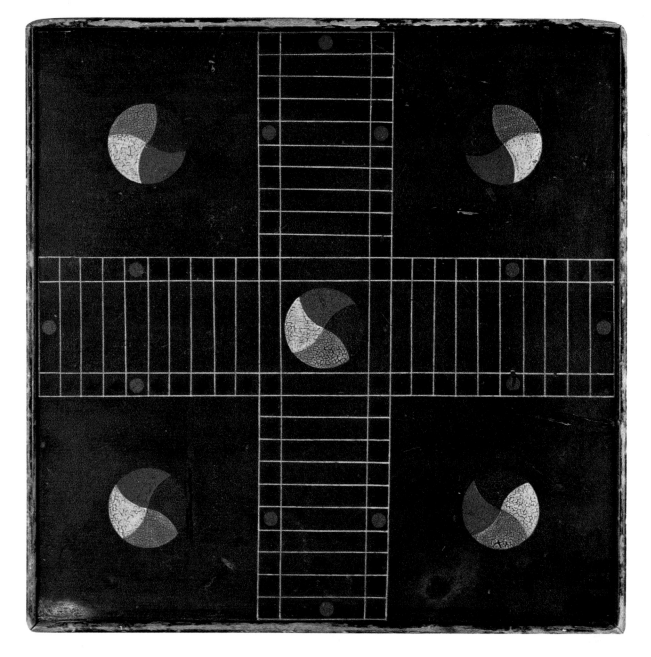

112.
Parcheesi Game-Board
Québec
Late nineteenth century
Painted wood
67.5 x 66.5 x 2.5 cm
Sharpe Coll., CCFCS 77-1202

Parcheesi (pachisi) is a traditional game
that was played as early as the sixth
century in India, although other early
versions of the game-board have also
been discovered among the Persians,
Iberians and Aztecs. The name is
derived from the Sanskrit word *pachis*,
meaning "twenty-five", the highest roll
of the original cowrie-shell dice.
Parcheesi became particularly popular
in Europe during the nineteenth
century, when it was known as "ludo",
and in variations such as "royal ludo".
Many Canadian boards, such as this
one, were handmade and decorated in
the folk manner.

113.
Checker Game
André Bourgault,
Saint-Jean–Port-Joli, Québec
ca. 1930
Painted wood
223 x 200 x 16 cm
CCFCS 78-408

To inform the public, the traditional
craftsman generally hung on his shop a
sign illustrating one aspect or another of
his craft. Made of painted wood, this
sign decorated the Bourgault sculptors'
shop in about the 1930s, and then
served as an advertisement for an
antique store. It illustrates a common
scene of earlier days, the checker game.
The lifelike quality of the figures and
the quiet humour of the scene make it a
most appealing work. It bears the
signature of André Bourgault.

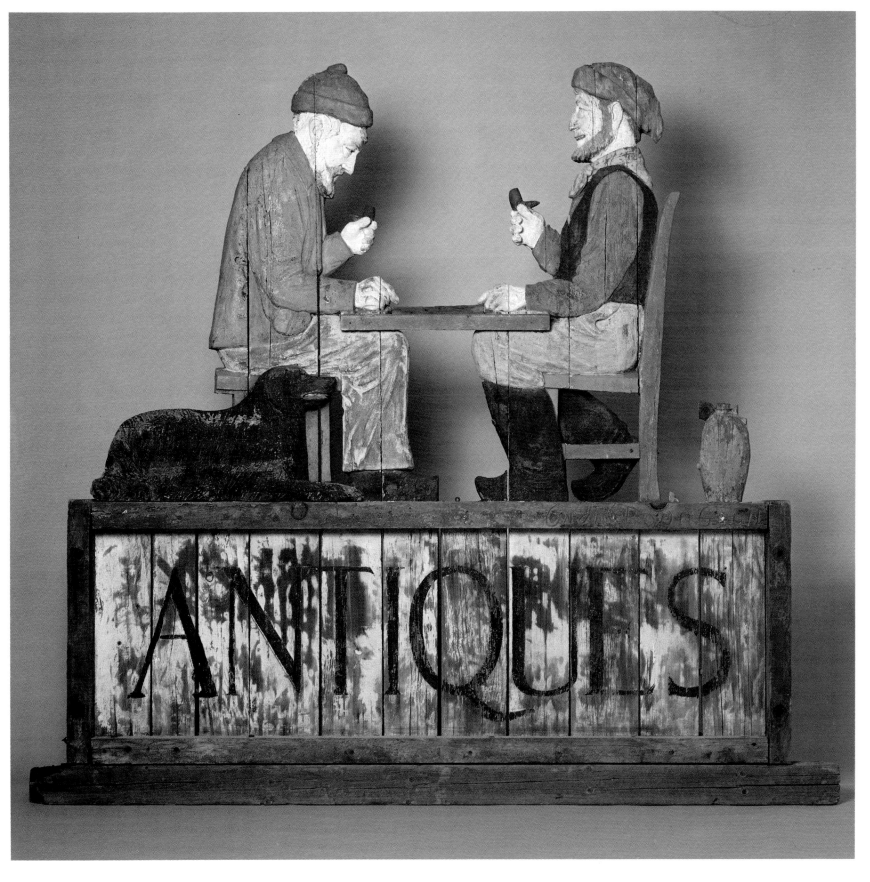

114.
"Le Beaujolais"
Jeanne Thomarat,
Duck Lake, Saskatchewan
1976
Oil on canvas
73 x 58 x 4.5 cm
CCFCS 79-590

Homesteading with her family in Saskatchewan around the turn of the century, young Jeanne Thomarat dreamt of returning permanently to her life of happiness and beauty in France. As time passed, the possibility became more remote and the memories dearer. In 1952 she began to paint from these memories places that were "not busy… peaceful, places where you would like to be with someone you love." Although she painted things the way she remembered them, she felt unrestricted by any particular realism in colour or detail, maintaining that "when you paint you can make it as nice as you want."

115.
"Panicking Horses"
Jahan Maka, Flin Flon, Manitoba
1975–79
Oil on canvas
99.5 x 69 x 4 cm
CCFCS 79-319

After retiring from a working life on the farms and in the forests and mines of Western Canada, Jahan Maka began to record his memories in paintings. That was in the early 1970s, forty years after coming to Canada from Lithuania. But memories of his homeland, the First World War and the Russian Revolution remained strong. In this painting, a group of riderless cavalry horses gallops over a bridge from Lithuania to Poland, while the Maka family escapes the fighting by hiding in a barge.

116.
"The Capture of Batoche"
D. Cam(p)bell, Brockville, Ontario
Early twentieth century
Oil on canvas
95.5 x 72.5 x 4.5 cm
CCFCS 78-589

At the battle of Batoche on 12 May 1885, Canadian militia units under Major General Frederick Middleton defeated the Métis nation. The artist is thought to have fought with the government forces and been wounded, but his painting was probably taken from a lithograph published in the *Canadian Pictorial and Illustrated War News* (30 May 1885, p. 68). Battle memorials in the form of descriptive paintings have a long history in Europe, a tradition that has been carried on in Canada.

THE CAPTURE OF BATOCHE

117.
"La chasse-galerie"
Fernand Thifault,
Saint-Adelphe, Québec
1977
House paint on canvas
175.5 x 128.5 x 2.5 cm
CCFCS 81-202

A carpenter by trade, Fernand Thifault spends his leisure time painting portraits and illustrating legends. This painting depicts "La chasse-galerie", a well-known Québec legend. Woodcutters leave their camp to go and celebrate in the village; the trip is made in a flying canoe propelled by the power of the devil; but on the return trip one of the travellers does something forbidden and the canoe becomes stranded at the top of a spruce tree. The figures in this painting are all familiar inhabitants of Saint-Adelphe, adding a touch of humour to the legend. The artist has given himself a pseudonym by changing the spelling of his name on the canvas.

118.
Louis Cyr
Joliette County, Québec
Early twentieth century
Painted wood
39 x 16.5 x 16.5 cm
Sharpe Coll., CCFCS 81-317

Louis Cyr lived from 1863 to 1912. A native of Saint-Cyprien in Napierville County, he was recognized as the strongest man in the world until he met his match in a man named Décarie in 1906. According to his biographers, Louis Cyr set several records that have never been equalled. He has passed into legend as the strongest man of all time. This statuette shows him in his favourite stance, his arms crossed over his powerful chest, legs spread apart and feet planted firmly on the ground.

119.
Leda and the Swan
Collins Eisenhauer,
Union Square, Nova Scotia
1975
Painted wood
21.5 x 21 x 12.5 cm
CCFCS 77-386

Birds were Collins Eisenhauer's favourite subject in his early sculptures. It is possible that the artist was inspired by the Greek myth of Zeus changing himself into a swan to seduce Leda. But the artist was probably attracted above all by the sculptural beauty of the swan and was prompted by his own erotic sense of humour.

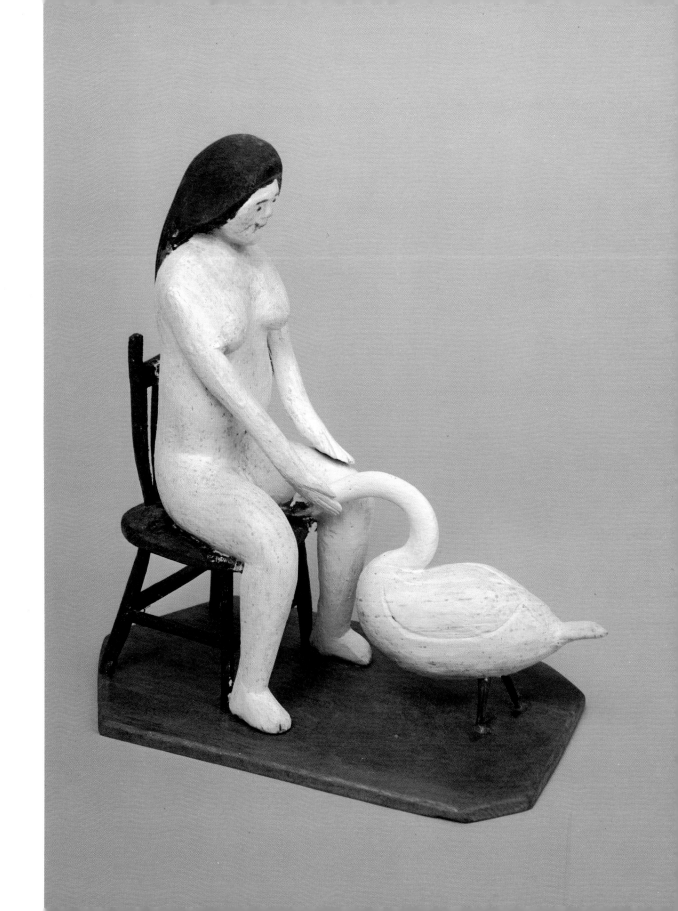

120.
The Stork
Billy Andrews, Bradford, Ontario
ca. 1950
Painted wood, cloth
27 x 19.5 x 11.5 cm
CCFCS 77-487

This figurine illustrates the well-known legend of the stork delivering the newborn infant to the family. Realistic, with a touch of humour, it mirrors the personality of the artist himself: "I'm just an ordinary man, and I'm using the talent that was given to me for life." The perfect detail and soft shades of colour make the carving a work of exquisite charm; it reveals the artist's attachment to tradition and his love of nature, particularly birds.

121.
The Fox and the Stork
Richelieu County, Québec
Mid-twentieth century
Wool and cotton on jute cloth
95 x 57 cm
Sharpe Coll., CCFCS 77-583

Classic works of French literature, La Fontaine's fables are also part of the popular heritage passed down by word of mouth from generation to generation. This rug illustrates the fable entitled "The Fox and the Stork". The perspective is striking. The pink background gives the entire work the same air of enchantment often found in oral tradition.

122.
Vide-sac
John Robert Goyer,
Brownsburg, Québec
1975
Basswood
Traveller: 121.5 x 49 x 7 cm
Lumberjack: 122 x 56 x 7 cm
Tree: 152.5 x 69 x 15.5 cm
CCFCS 81-332 (1–3)

This three-piece work, in which the faces were inspired by old portraits of habitants, was originally to have been part of a picture containing some twenty figures and representing the place-name "Vide-sac" (empty sack), applied locally to the town of Lachute. It is said that habitants from Saint-Hermes and Sainte-Scholastique came to cut wood at Lachute, arriving with a sackful of victuals to last the week. As soon as they had run out of supplies, however, they had to return home. Hence, the name Vide-sac, which has been preserved in local tradition. Today, a district, a street and even a pub in the area carry the name.

Commitment

The folk art of commitment is the art of allegiance and constancy, in which the artists display their devotion to loved ones, to their community, their nation and their God. By and large, these declarations are symbolic, their directness camouflaged by the use of widely understood symbols that tend to stir emotion rather than memory.

Icons, a term now used to refer to secular as well as religious objects, capture the spirit of what they depict, and remind the viewer repeatedly of his loyalties. While an icon may symbolize a saint or a religious belief, it may also be an object that evokes an emotional response to the joys and sorrows of the past. This is the case with the so-called ethnic icon, an object of cultural allegiance, which is often placed in a special area of the home.

While religious symbols are perhaps those most easily recognized, the folk art of commitment also contains symbols from other areas of life, such as love, work and pride in family. The heart, perhaps the most frequently used symbol in all of folk art, represents the true spirit of commitment, and is therefore the most common motif in love tokens made by men and women when separation must be endured.

Family Records

(Numbers 123–124)

Framed family records were popular throughout the nineteenth century in Eastern Canada. With the burgeoning interest in draftsmanship and calligraphy, what had once been hidden inside the family Bible was now hung on the wall. Originally, family records noted births, marriages and deaths.

As the century wore on, however, the Victorian fascination with death took the upper hand and we find commemorative records becoming more and more prevalent, incorporating a biblical or sentimental phrase, a lock of the deceased's hair, and finally, before the tradition spent itself in the early twentieth century, photographs of the departed.

123.
Family Record
Lunenburg County, Nova Scotia
Early twentieth century
Ink on paper
58 x 55 x 2 cm
CCFCS 77-732

124.
Family Record
Newcombville, Nova Scotia
Late nineteenth century
Ink and watercolour on paper
39 x 32 x 2 cm
CCFCS 80-414

125.
"Ukrainian Girl:
A Daughter of the Pioneers"
Molly Lenhardt, Melville, Saskatchewan
ca. 1970
Oil on canvas
84 x 58.5 x 3.5 cm
CCFCS 80-210

Many of Molly Lenhardt's paintings
have been inspired by the spirit and
sense of justice of her father, who
struggled much of his life to improve
the conditions of poverty-stricken
Ukrainian peasants in both the Old
Country and Canada. Her pictures tend
toward the iconic, depicting values and
ideas more than historical detail. In this
painting, the artist symbolically portrays
the dilemma of the second-generation
Canadian raised in a new society but
also living in the parents' past. The
handkerchief in the girl's right hand
suggests sorrow and regret for the past,
and the flowers the hope and promise of
the future. Ultimately Molly Lenhardt's
concern is with Canada, " a new
culture, our own Canadian culture, not
one borrowed from elsewhere".

126.
Orange Lodge Chair
Fredericton, New Brunswick
Late nineteenth century
Painted wood, metal, fabric
110 x 57.5 x 54 cm
CCFCS 76-483

The image of King William III, Prince of Orange, associates this chair with the Orange Association, which promoted Protestant religious freedom and celebrated "King Billy's" victory in 1690 in the Battle of the Boyne. The British army brought Orangeism to the colonies around 1800, and several lodges operated in the Fredericton area. The symbols on this chair suggest that it served more than one ceremonial function. It could have been used by the lodge chaplain and by candidates who were being "exalted" through the various lodge degrees, which were based upon moral virtues and identified by biblical symbols. Symbols from three degrees are present:

Royal Blue Degree

a) Candles:
twelve pins on the top of the chair support twelve candles representing the Apostles;

b) Star:
the Star of the East, which marked the birthplace of Jesus;

c) Blue paint.

Royal Arch Purple Degree

a) Two small candle-holders;

b) Pillars and arches with keystones;

c) Jacob's ladder:
three rungs for "Faith, Hope and Charity";

d) Coffin;

e) Serpent.

Royal Black Institution
—all the remaining symbols.

119

127.
Mountie Quilt
Beth Craig, Delta, Ontario
1975
Appliquéd cotton
265 x 170 cm
CCFCS 77-327

This quilt was made to honour the
Royal Canadian Mounted Police. Beth
Craig was inspired to the task because
she felt that children should be taught
that Mounties have exceptional qualities
—knowledge and love of nature, bravery
and fairness. Part cowboy, part Boy
Scout and part soldier, the Mountie is
the symbolic embodiment of the highest
Canadian values. In tradition and
popular imagination, he has become
one of the most enduring icons of
Canadian life.

128.
Coatrack
Howard Milne, Sundridge, Ontario
Early twentieth century
Painted wood, metal
104 x 47.5 x 29.5 cm
CCFCS 74-594

Howard Milne was a farmer and trapper
who made extra money as a sign painter.
His lifelong hobby was painting and
carving. A deeply religious man, he felt
strongly about his country's allegiances
and about personal friendship,
as the flags, clasped hands, and national
animals on this coatrack testify.

129.
"Sailors Grave"
Nova Scotia
ca. 1945
Painted wood
46 x 38 x 2 cm
CCFCS 81-129

This plaque stems from a long tradition of sailors' memorials, and commemorates the men and vessels of the merchant marine that were lost during the Second World War. The letter "V" was of course the Allies' sign for victory, and the Morse code equivalent (. . . −) was used by the radio operators of the merchant marine as a warm-up signal, alerting others to an upcoming message. The Morse "V" was also used by commercial newscasters, usually in the form of the first four notes of Beethoven's Fifth Symphony.

130.
Veteran
Ontario
Twentieth century
Painted wood, fabric
35.5 x 10 x 8 cm
CCFCS 74-269

While this carving may memorialize a particular individual, the defiant head, barrel-chested columnar body, round-toed no-nonsense shoes, and generalized uniform symbolize Canadian veterans as a whole. It is not only the symbols of affiliation—flag, badge and uniform—but the figure's solid bearing that gives this creation the iconic quality of invincibility and pride.

131.
Dove on Bomb
Cambridge, Ontario
1918
Painted wood
57 x 26 x 20.5 cm
CCFCS 77-460

This sculpture was made by an employee of Goldie and McColloch Company Limited of Galt (now Cambridge), Ontario, which made artillery shells during the First World War. Symbolizing the triumph of peace over strife, it was part of the company's Armistice Day parade float in 1918.

132.
"Dependable Protection"
Stratford, Ontario
Mid-twentieth century
Wool on canvas
119 x 56 cm
CCFCS 76-231

The hooked rug often depicts domestic scenes, nature and objects of whimsy. In this case, events in the outside world have impressed themselves on the artist's imagination. The rug becomes not just a decorative object but a statement of belief in the power of British arms to protect the homeland and its allies. With the Union Jack as a backdrop, the bulldog stands on a rock, and fighter aircraft and battleships patrol in the distance. The symbolism is direct and powerful, matching the anxiety and dread of threatened invasion and conquest.

133.
"God Bles Our Home"
Weber family, Young, Saskatchewan
Twentieth century
Painted wood
62.5 x 39.5 x 3.5 cm
CCFCS 79-609

"God Bless Our Home" has probably been one of the most popular icons in Canadian homes, whether embroidered, painted or printed. This one is unusual in that it has been cut from wood, probably following a predrawn pattern. The piece shows greater woodworking skill than spelling ability.

134–136.
Corn Dollies
Everett Thompson, Carman, Manitoba
ca. 1980
Straw
CCFCS
82-130: 60 x 13 x 11 cm
82-131: 41 x 25 x 3.5 cm
82-132: 56 x 24 x 4 cm

Certain folk-art forms grow directly out of a traditional belief. In many cultures, the spirit of the grain lives in the field, but dies when the last sheaf is cut. In order to preserve her so that she may be reborn the following spring, the last sheaf is braided into a recognizable figure and used as an enhancer of fertility. Everett Thompson learned the craft from his mother-in-law, who had learned to make corn dollies from a native of Britain, where the custom is well known. Although "corn dolly" is the usual name, oat, wheat or rye straw may also be used to make the figures, which are also known as kern babies, harvest queens and mother sheaf.

124

137.
Resurrection Cane
Abitibi County, Québec
Nineteenth century
Wood
85 x 4.5 cm
CCFCS 79-1638

This cane is a striking example of the meeting of two cultures and especially the meeting of two systems of belief. In all likelihood of Iroquois origin, it combines symbols of traditional Iroquois mythology with those of Christianity. The serpent coiling toward the left, aquatic animals like the turtle, as well as the dogwood near the pommel are all ambivalent Iroquois symbols of death and new life. Christ crucified, surrounded by the instruments of His passion, is the symbol of resurrection. The cross, in keeping with a widespread Québec tradition, is surmounted by a cock, the symbol of vigilance and resurrection. The common hope for new life is clearly illustrated at the top of the cane by the dogwood, "Great Tree of Light", topped by a cock.

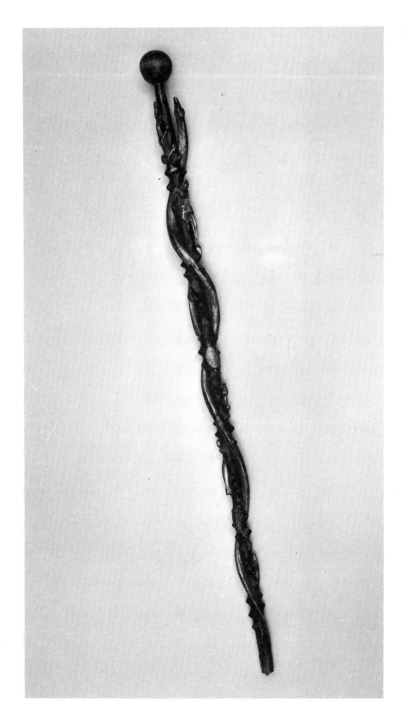

138.
Tree of Life
Attributed to a Mrs. Robert,
Saint-Jean-Baptiste-de-Rouville, Québec
1890
Wool on jute cloth
104 x 101 cm
Sharpe Coll., CCFCS 77-585

The tree of life is a universal symbol dating back to ancient times. It is reproduced in this rug according to the Christian interpretation. The tree with seven roots represents eternal life nourished by the seven sacraments. It is flanked by two crosses mounted on steeples and two cups, decorated with human faces, from which spring bouquets of flowers, symbols perhaps of secular life. The two black horses on a red background may represent fortitude. Two chimerical animals occupy heaven. The work is dated 10 December 1890.

Adam and Eve
(Numbers 139–141)

The story of Adam and Eve cast out from Paradise after committing the original sin has inspired a great number of artists, heirs of the Judaeo-Christian tradition. In Europe, painters, sculptors and all types of anonymous craftsmen have immortalized this story from the first pages of the Bible, which seeks to explain the presence of evil in the world. This age-old tradition was brought to America by the first European settlers and inspires folk artists even today. The following three examples, through the variety of the media used, the regional flavour of the tradition, and the diversity of the interpretations of the story, provide an indication of the scope of the phenomenon.

139.
"Adam and Eve"
Henrietta Dyer,
Metcalfe Township, Middlesex County, Ontario
1889
Wool and silk on canvas
53 x 53 x 5.5 cm
CCFCS 77-451

This piece of embroidery, simple in design and uneven in execution, is undoubtedly the work of a novice. It bears witness to the strict adherence to religious tradition and to the practical educational methods of the period.

127

140.
Adam and Eve
Philippe Roy, Saint-Philémon, Québec
1975–80
Painted wood
Adam: 30.5 x 11 x 10 cm
Eve: 27.5 x 11 x 10.5 cm
Tree: 34 x 11 x 11 cm
CCFCS 80-162; 80-163; 80-164

The candour and simplicity of the
deeply religious folk artist who enjoyed
carving the mysteries of the Christian
faith are reflected in this simple scene.

141.
"Adam and Eve"
Collins Eisenhauer,
Union Square, Nova Scotia
ca. 1975
Painted wood
54 x 43 x 33 cm
CCFCS 77-378

In this scene the artist proposes a folk
interpretation of original sin that
borders on irreverence for traditional
religious teachings.

142.
High Mass
Sainte-Rosalie, Québec
Twentieth century
Painted wood
54 x 32 x 29 cm
Sharpe Coll., CCFCS 77-992

This piece shows a priest saying high mass with a deacon and subdeacon. The architecture is rococo, a popular style in traditional Québec churches. The reredos is formed of pieces of wood glued together, to which the artisan has added twisted columns on either side. The piece is topped by a cross with a radiant sun at its centre and flanked by two birds facing each other. On the altar front, hidden by the celebrants, is the Last Supper. The priest can be made to pivot by manipulating a lever located under the altar steps.

143.
The Holy Family
Near Caughnawaga, Québec
Early nineteenth century
Painted wood
83.5 x 74 x 14 cm
CCFCS 76-191

Christian tradition usually depicts the Holy Family on a less tragic day. This scene of the crucified Christ with Mary and Joseph has remarkable evocative power. It is an example of the age-old universal tradition of accompanying instruction, whether religious or secular, with images that vividly reinforce the message.

144.
The Crucifixion
Philippe Roy, Saint-Philémon, Québec
ca. 1960
Painted wood, hair, thorns
Sharpe Coll., CCFCS
77-1077: 77 x 38 x 11 cm
77-1078: 77 x 38 x 13.5 cm
77-1079: 76.5 x 38 x 11 cm

Philippe Roy led a simple, secluded life with his sister in a very isolated house. He had a special rapport with nature and was deeply religious. Mr. Roy began carving while working in a lumber camp in his youth. It was not until thirty years later, because of illness, that he began to sell his carvings to pickers. He liked to carve the Christian mysteries, especially Christ on the cross. Using only discarded pieces of wood, a simple penknife, emery paper and leftover paint, he nevertheless was capable of heightening realism with a few details. In this work, the figures of Christ and the two thieves have human hair, and Christ's crown is made of real thorns.

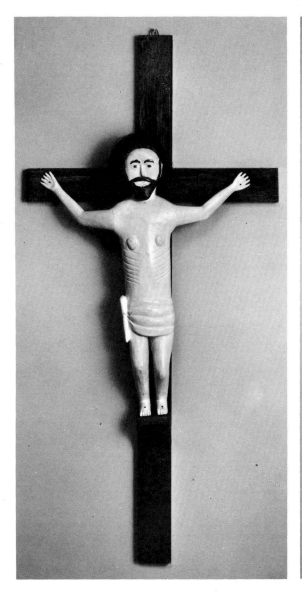  

145.
Calvary
Philippe Roy, Saint-Philémon, Québec
1978
Painted wood
Crucifixion: 57 x 43 x 19 cm
Cock: 31 x 20 x 10 cm
CCFCS 81-321 (1–6)

The later works of Philippe Roy generally convey the modesty and serenity of the artist himself. This remarkable Calvary illustrates the artist's religious convictions.

The serpent in the tree is the cause of Christ's death, and Joseph has been added to the scene because it is important to unite the Holy Family. The ball in the cage surmounted by the cock represents Earth held captive through Peter's denial of Christ, the symbol of all the rejections of mankind.

146.
The Holy Spirit
Philippe Roy, Saint-Philémon, Québec
1945–50
Painted wood, plastic
42 x 30 x 14 cm
Sharpe Coll., CCFCS 81-316

This dove represents the Holy Spirit. A
concrete symbol of divine grace, it used
to hang in the artist's home.

147.
The Crown of Thorns
Thomas Brisson, Saint-Gervais, Québec
ca. 1945
Cedar
35 (diam.) x 9.5 cm
CCFCS 80-624

This artisan likes to demonstrate his
skill by carving meticulous works whose
themes are often drawn from tradition.
He made this crown of thorns to pass
the time during the Christmas holidays
before returning to his work at a lumber
camp. It hung on the bedroom wall as a
reminder of Christ's passion.

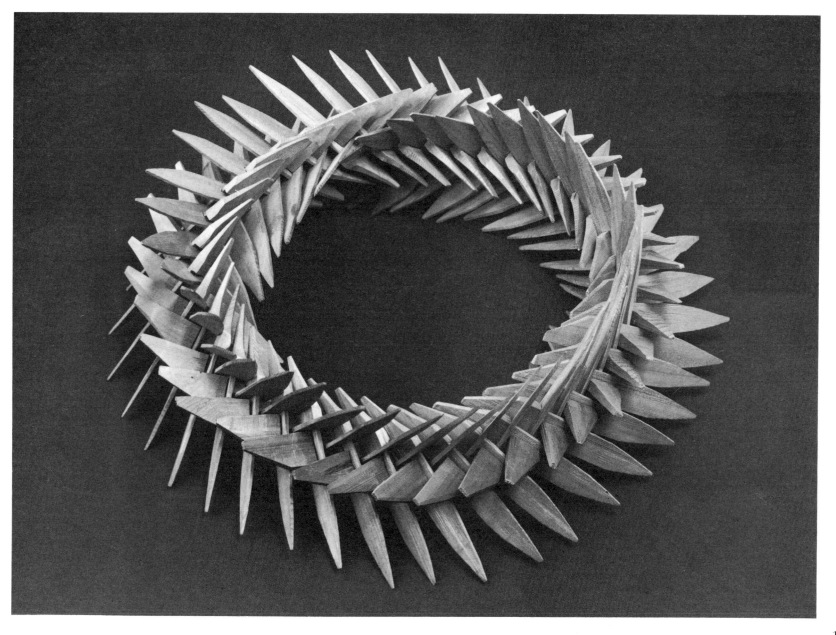

148.
Memento of Confirmation
Québec
Twentieth century
Wood, photograph
24.5 x 19.5 x 3 cm
CCFCS 74-595

The sacrament of Confirmation is doubtless associated with the rites of initiation marking the transition from childhood to adulthood. Confirmation was an occasion for expensive festivities, especially among Latin peoples. The souvenir photograph was a means of recording the event. This one has been placed in an ornate frame bearing carved reliefs of two ciboria flanking, among other motifs, the cross, anchor and heart, symbolizing faith, hope and charity respectively. The inscription on the back of the photograph reads "Mell. Alexendrine Boisvenu 1911 F. 18".

149.
"Benedictus"
Saint-Ours, Québec
Twentieth century
Hardwood
28 x 17 x 5 cm
Sharpe Coll., CCFCS 77-1320

Crossing oneself with holy water is a rite that symbolizes the passage from the secular world to the sacred. This mould was used to make plaster fonts. It bears the effigy of an angel giving a blessing and the inscription "Benedictus". The basin was formed by inserting in the opening a piece of shaped wood and removing it once the plaster was set.

Sugar Moulds

(Numbers 150–158)

The springtime task of making maple sugar, with its varied moulds attesting to tradition, ingenuity and imagination, called on symbolic references to the Easter mystery and the awakening of love. Sugar moulds date back to the second half of the nineteenth century.

150.
"Je vous em"
(I Luv You)
Saint-Narcisse, Lotbinière County, Québec
Twentieth century
Wood
22.5 x 11 x 5 cm (assembled)
Sharpe Coll., CCFCS 77-1293

At one time, a young man would offer a sugar loaf in the shape of a heart to his sweetheart to express his love. This mould is particularly explicit. The two surfaces are different. One has two hearts separated by a triangle; this motif may have been merely decorative or may have represented a love blessed by God. There is also a radiant sun surrounded by crosses, as well as the traditional diamond-shaped motif that, like the heart, symbolizes good luck and happiness. On the other surface, two hearts are upheld by the misspelled inscription "Cher dem/oielle je/vous em/boucou" (Dear lady, I love you very much), some of the letters being inscribed upside-down. Underneath is carved another radiant sun.

151.
Six Hearts
Québec
Late nineteenth to early twentieth century
Wood
71.5 x 8 x 3 cm
Sharpe Coll., CCFCS 77-1337

Made up of two pieces of wood held together with nails, this mould has two series of three hearts, all pointing toward the centre. Each heart has a different motif carved on it.

152.
Two Fluted Hearts
Québec
Mid-nineteenth century
Wood
41 x 9 x 4 cm (assembled)
Sharpe Coll., CCFCS 77-1299

This mould consists of a piece of wood on which are engraved two hearts decorated with crosses and radiant suns. The base has 5 pinned tenon joints, over which the three mortised pieces are fitted.

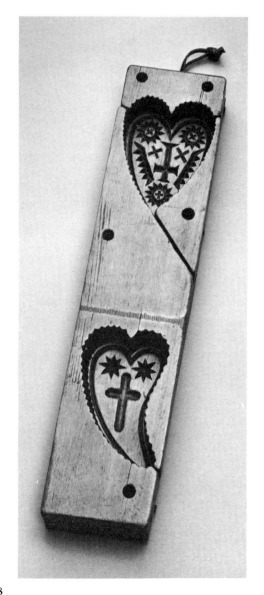

153.
Village Church
Québec
Late nineteenth century
Wood
30 x 27 x 19 cm (assembled)
CFFCS 75-904

Made of six pieces of wood held
together by two pinned tenons and nine
split dowels, this mould forms the sugar
into the shape of a village church. The
façade bears the inscription "1894 IHS",
and "POV" is inscribed on the apse.

154.
The Paschal Lamb
Saint-Antoine-sur-Richelieu, Québec
Late nineteenth century
Wood
42.5 x 13.5 x 7 cm
Sharpe Coll., CCFCS 77-1287

The carving on this sugar mould shows
the paschal lamb recumbent on the
cross above a hot grill. In the upper
corners are what appear to be the rods
with metal balls used for the scourging
of Christ. The two moulds are carved
from a single piece of wood.

155.
The Cross
Québec
Late nineteenth century
Wood
21 x 15 x 5.5 cm
CCFCS 72-833

This mould is in the form of a
monumental cross incised with some of
the instruments of the Passion. The
initials "GA" are carved on the base.

156.
Fish
Québec
Late nineteenth century
Wood
29.5 x 11.5 x 7 cm (closed)
Sharpe Coll., CCFCS 77-1332 (1, 2)

Made of two pieces of wood held together by four pins, this mould represents a fish. It is known that primitive Christian art, which has been perpetuated in Christian religious iconography, often represents Christ as a fish. The Greek term *ikhthus* "fish" corresponds to the initials of *Iesous Khristos Theou Uios Soter* "Jesus Christ, Son of God, the Saviour".

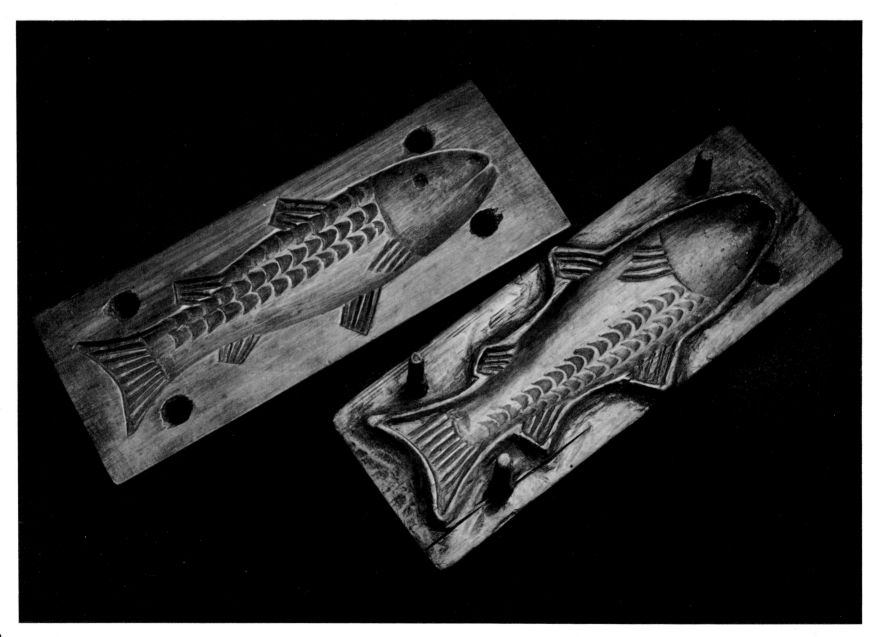

157.
The Cock
Québec
Early twentieth century
Wood
21 x 17.5 x 5 cm
Sharpe Coll., CCFCS 77-1326

The cock is another recurring theme of
the Easter season, perhaps a reference
to the cock in the gospel account of
Peter's denial of Christ. This mould
probably included another similar
piece, which would have been fastened
to it with pegs at the four corners to
make a fully formed bird.

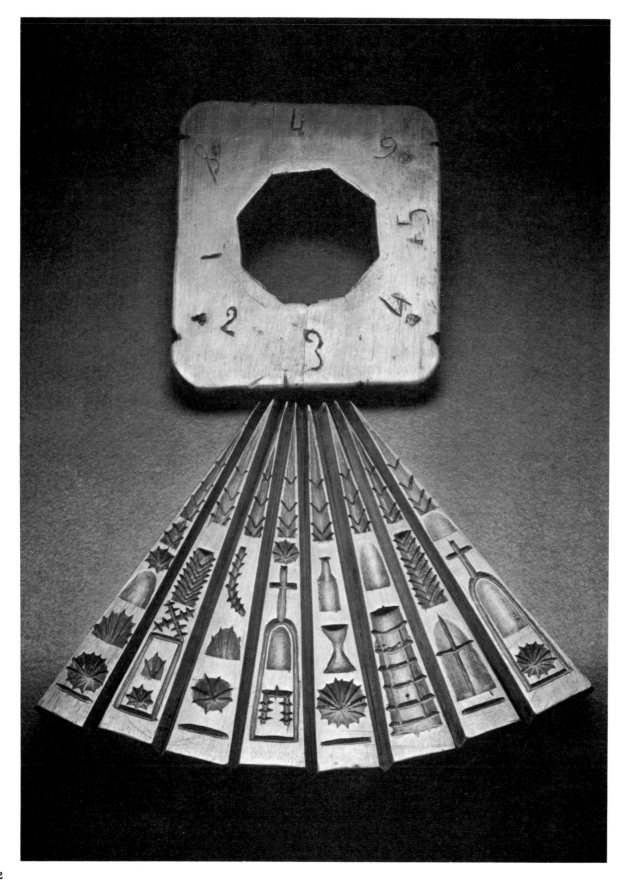

158.
The Whimsical Cone
Québec
Twentieth century
Wood
23 x 20 x 16.5 cm (assembled)
Sharpe Coll., CCFCS 77-1298

This sugar mould is an example of ingenuity and imagination. For easy assembly, the numbers inscribed on the base correspond to those found on the outer face of each of the eight triangular sections. Various motifs—niches, crosses, suns, shells, bottles, hourglasses, towers—are carved on the inside of the sections. The point of the cone was held together by a string passed under the minuscule wooden tenons set into the sharply pointed summit of each section.

159.
Courting Mirror
Lunenburg County, Nova Scotia
Early twentieth century
Painted wood, mirror
32.5 x 32 x 2 cm
CCFCS 77-166

Many folk-art objects have multiple
layers of cultural meaning. A
superficially simple object may have a
specific function, but may also represent
an orthodox belief system or
superstition. Mirrors such as this one
were occasionally presented as courting
gifts. Aside from being pleasingly
decorative, they were a declaration of
the values of the maker's community.
The anchor represents hope, the cross
faith, and the heart-shaped mirror
charity or love. Mirror fragments
are also used as a folk religious device,
inset in gifts to ward off the evil eye.

160.
Stay Busk
Ontario
1796
Wood
26.5 x 4.5 x 1.5 cm
NMM History Division E-8

In the latter part of the seventeenth and
again in the late eighteenth century,
fashion decreed small waists, and
women's clothing featured corsets with
wood or whalebone stays. This gave
occasion to suitors to decorate with chip
or scratch carving special stays, or
busks, for their sweethearts to wear. The
most commonly carved motifs were
twin hearts, lovebirds, flowers and
leaves, and geometric designs of various
types. The busks were often incised
with dates, initials and declarations of
love. As this particular item was
obtained from descendants of
Lieutenant Governor John Graves
Simcoe, it may have been made in
Canada or at least worn here, possibly
by some member of his family.

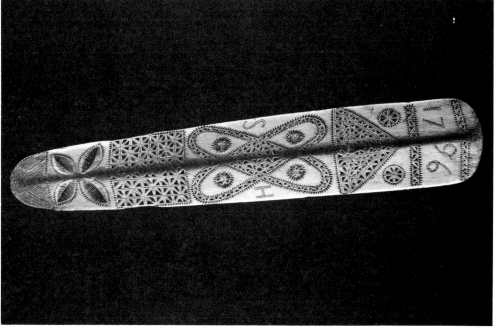

161

162

163

164

144

Handkerchiefs

(Numbers 161–165)

Decorative handkerchiefs have a long history in Europe, not only as items of personal use, but as an intimate part of her apparel that a woman might offer to a sweetheart as a sign of commitment and affection. The Hutterites have preserved this tradition into the twentieth century.

161.
Handkerchief
Alberta
Mid-twentieth century
Embroidered cotton
45 x 40 cm
CCFCS 79–489

162.
Handkerchief
Wallman family, Leask, Alberta
1926
Embroidered cotton
40 x 40 cm
CCFCS 77–823

163.
Handkerchief
Sara Entz, Alberta
1932
Embroidered cotton
40 x 38 cm
CCFCS 79–490

164.
Handkerchief
Annie Stahl, Alberta
Mid-twentieth century
Embroidered cotton
40 x 40 cm
CCFCS 79–491

165.
Handkerchief
Mary Hofer, Alberta
1944
Embroidered cotton
40 x 38 cm
CCFCS 79–865

166.
Love-Spoons
Ontario
Nineteenth century
Wood
95 x 6 x 5 cm
CCFCS 73–574

The custom of transforming ordinary objects into ceremonial and presentational courtship tokens is of long standing in European folk culture. Chained spoons carved from a single piece of wood date back to at least the seventeenth century. The close fit of the two spoons may be a reference to the intimacies of the marriage bed, while the chain is probably a symbol of the unbreakable bonds of matrimony.

This pair of love-spoons, according to available information and comparison with similar examples, probably was made by a carver of North-European, possibly Norwegian, origin.

167.

Love-Letter Box

Maritime Provinces

Nineteenth century

Wood

25.5 x 17 x 4 cm

CCFCS 79–810

Incised and chip-carved boxes made of
wood and fashioned in the shape of
books were in vogue in seventeenth-
century Europe as snuff boxes.
Canadian boxes of this type are usually
larger and were made to contain small
valuables, a prayer-book, or even spruce
gum. They are commonly associated
with lumberjacks, who carved them for
their sweethearts. The carving on this
love-letter box indicates that they were
also known among seafarers.

168.
Marriage Quilt
Mary Morris, Elgin, Ontario
1825
Cotton, linen
200 x 185 cm
R. McKendry Coll., CCFCS 79–237

Quilting bees were sometimes courting occasions, with men invited to observe the deft fingers of their intended; some even participated. A special, highly decorated quilt intended for the marriage bed often became the single most important piece in a girl's hope chest. This marriage quilt dates from 1825, and contains European-influenced motifs in the embroidered designs.

Mary Morris made the piece for her hope chest at the age of fourteen, but never used it; tragically, she was born with a club-foot and never married. Nor was the quilt used by subsequent owners.

169.
Bunk Mat
Lunenburg County, Nova Scotia
ca. 1900
Painted canvas
104.5 x 56 cm
G. Ferguson Coll., CCFCS 81–315

Sailcloth mats decorated with thickly painted designs are found in Nova Scotia's Lunenburg County. They were made and used by sailors, who laid them on the floor beside their bunks aboard ship, although such mats have also been used as an inexpensive floor-covering in Maritime homes. The tradition probably dates no further back than the late nineteenth or early twentieth century. The clasped hands on this particular mat are a common motif, representing the spiritual unity of lovers—between the sailor on his ship and the loved one on shore.

170.
Love-Seat
Onésime Labrosse, Montebello, Québec
1909
Painted wood
100 x 99.5 x 57 cm
Lent by Raymond Labrosse,
Saint-André-Avellin, Québec

Onésime Labrosse was a "walker" for a lumber company, marking trees to be cut down, while his wife and thirteen children tended the family farm at Montebello. During his long absences he used his spare time to make this gift, which celebrates the strength of his marriage bond. The clasped-hands design and the names of man and wife were carved with axe and pocketknife. The making of such love-seats, with a love token carved or painted on the back-support, is a tradition known in France since at least the eighteenth century.

171.
Embracing Couple
Clément Cinq-Mars, Longueuil, Québec
ca. 1960
Painted wood
14 x 6 x 4 cm
CCFCS 70–101

The *Embracing Couple* is one of many three-dimensional carvings created by Clément Cinq-Mars as part of a lifelong hobby. His keen observations of people and their peculiarities have been expressed with only a pocketknife and a feeling for wood, born of his trade as a carpenter. After his retirement, Mr. Cinq-Mars began to experiment with more-complex carved miniatures as well as with paint and canvas.

Fantasy

Of the many characteristics of folk art, adherence to tradition and established techniques is the most widespread. In this section, however, the emphasis is placed upon the personal fantasies of folk artists, resulting in the choice of pieces that at times go well beyond what has been viewed as folk art. These pieces display innovation and unpredictability, affecting their form, technique and subject-matter.

A concept often connected with fantasy in folk art is whimsy, and indeed many of these pieces are whimsical, reflecting the capricious or fanciful ideas of their creators. The logical extension of these themes is humour, resulting in pieces such as the monkey bellhop, a creature whose gigantic stride mirrors the urgency of his calling and reinforces the label on his suitcase, "We are never late."

Other works in this section represent different fantasies. Some are overtly erotic, while others recount dreams of artistic vision in which the artist displays a personal conception of the world and its creatures. Eccentricity is a term often applied to this type of folk art, yet the realm of fantasy is appearing more frequently in the work of Canada's contemporary folk artists.

172.
Model Sleigh
Arthur L. Flett, Winnipeg, Manitoba
Mid-twentieth century
Painted wood, fabric, string
31 x 11 x 7 cm
CCFCS 79–332

Carvings of couples riding together have been popular with this artist. Here a pair wearing parkas ride in a sleigh with a "Just Marrid" sign on the rear. On one side is painted "Honey slow down", and on the other, "Honey, you are going too fast." The theme seems to involve a commonly held view about one aspect of married life: no sooner is the ceremony over than the bride begins criticizing her new husband's driving habits. Mr. Flett's tools are homemade and the ideas, he says, "have come out of my head".

173.
Fisherman and Wife
Philip Melvin, Ontario
1980
Painted wood
Fisherman: 72 x 18.5 x 8.5 cm
Wife: 65.5 x 19 x 12.5 cm
CCFCS 81–134; 81–135

Philip Melvin was born in La Manche,
Newfoundland, on April Fool's Day in
1938. He left there twenty-five years ago
and has not been back, but he evidently
still identifies strongly and humorously
with his birthplace. As he says, "They
call me the 'Man from La Manche'." Mr.
Melvin has worked in sawmills, oilfields
and on a chain gang, and has taken
whatever work came his way. He has
developed a philosophical outlook and
writes poetry and prose, often on
religious subjects. Of this pair of
carvings he says, "I made a man, made
a wife for the man, turned around for
five minutes, and look what happened!"

174.
Bathing Beauty with Dart
Lawrence Melanson,
Mill Village, Queens County,
Nova Scotia
1950
Painted wood, fabric
53 x 27 x 10 cm
G. Ferguson Coll., CCFCS 81–70

Still a carpenter, who carves in his spare time, Lawrence Melanson states simply, "I love to work with wood." After learning to carve while working in lumber camps in the 1940s and 50s, he created this bathing beauty from a pin-up calendar illustration. She originally held a towel between her upraised hands and was on a stand with an eight-day clock from a Cadillac automobile. The dart and the current stand were added by a later owner.

175.
Beach-Ball Blonde
Donald Boudreau, Digby, Nova Scotia
1977
Painted wood
33.5 x 21.5 x 12.5 cm
CCFCS 78–222

176.
Bathing Beauty
Donald Boudreau, Digby, Nova Scotia
1977
Painted wood
48.5 x 21 x 12.5 cm
CCFCS 81–369

Donald Boudreau has been working with wood for over thirty years. A resident of Nova Scotia's north shore, Mr. Boudreau opened a lumberyard several years ago, but finding that business tended to be slower in the winter months, he turned his hand to carving at the urging of friends. The two bathing figures are among the first he completed, although he has also created seagulls, whirligigs and other small carvings inspired by his Maritime background.

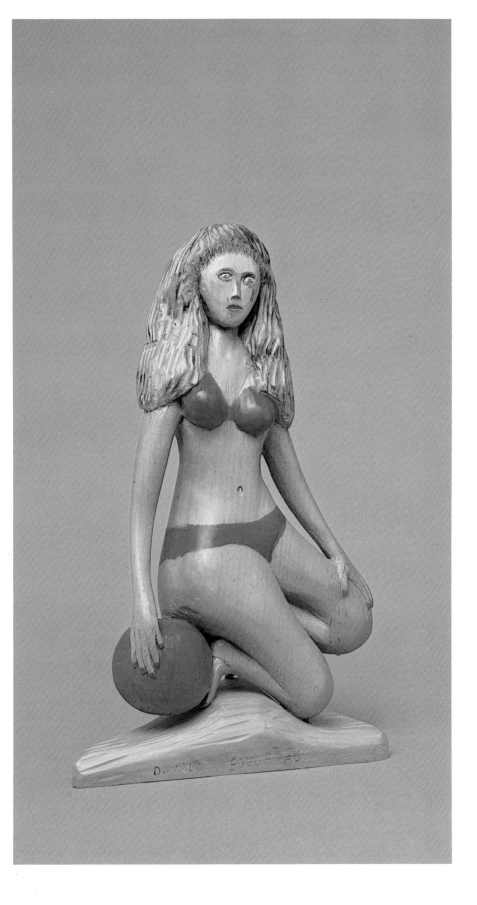

157

177.
"Venus"
Claude Pierre Luneau, Toronto, Ontario
1981
Painted wood
99 x 39 x 20 cm
CCFCS 01–131

Claude Luneau's interest in carving developed during his years as an art-gallery technician while building exhibit cases and seeing the works of art that went into them. Eventually he felt that he too had the ability and imagination to create. This sculpture was inspired by a poem that the artist has known for a long time. It begins, "On a mountain stands a lady", and ends, "All she needs is a fine young man." The winner of the wrestling match will be that young man.

178.
Sailor and Friends
Alma Baldwin, Big Bay Point, Ontario
ca. 1950
Painted cloth, cotton batting, nylon stockings
34 x 33 x 27 cm
CCFCS 78–58; 78–59; 78–60

These dolls are part of a large group caricaturing people that Alma Baldwin had known or observed during her active life. While bedridden during the years 1948 to 1952, she passed the time constructing her satirical universe of familiar types with astonishing skill and a sense of humour. War and snappy uniforms undoubtedly transformed many shy and circumspect lads into roving Don Juans, and this young sailor is no exception.

179.
Adam and Eve
Alphonse Grenier,
Saint-Jean-de-la-Lande, Beauce County,
Québec
1978
Painted wood
67 x 56.5 x 1.5 cm
CCFCS 80–133

Alphonse Grenier was concerned in his carvings with the social mores of the past as compared with those of the present. In this brightly painted lawn ornament, he was clearly alluding to the traditional scene of Adam and Eve in the Garden of Eden, but he placed them beside the Tree of Knowledge in modern dress. There is no apple or snake, and the tree is an evergreen, adding a distinct tongue-in-cheek flavour to the Fall of Man.

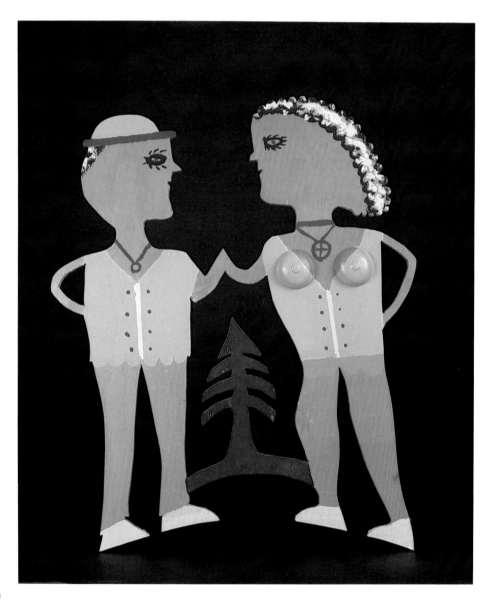

180.
The Lovers
William McClelland,
Port Greville, Nova Scotia
Mid-twentieth century
Painted wood
32 x 15 x 6 cm
CCFCS 77–306

Reminiscences and memories are the constant companions of sailors, woodsmen and others whose careers require lengthy absences from home. In the hands of folk artists, these thoughts often resulted in depictions of their houses, families, pets, and wives or sweethearts. Some of these last were gently romantic, others frankly erotic.

Captain William McClelland was a seafaring man, whose subjects ranged from model ships to human figures. *The Lovers* is a blend of both the romantic and the erotic, although the otherwise nude female figure sports a decorous pair of pink panties that might have been added later. Carved from a single piece of 2 x 6 pine, the figures were first shellacked and then painted.

181.
The Dance of Life
Ewald Rentz, Beardmore,
Ontario
ca. 1975
Painted wood
26.5 x 17.5 x 15.5 cm
CCFCS 80–116

Distinctly impressionistic in tone, *The Dance of Life* suggests lovers in a passionate embrace, through the use of natural "found" objects, wood putty and two paint colours. Two tree burls fastened together form the figures.

182.
Turkey
Ewald Rentz, Beardmore, Ontario
ca. 1975
Painted wood, fungi, leather
92 x 51 x 35 cm
CCFCS 80–115

Ewald Rentz maintains that he cannot "make" art; he can only "complete" what he finds in nature. His turkey combines a burl as the body and a large fan-fungus for the tail, with other smaller fungi nailed on the neck. Strips of leather decorate the legs and breast and serve as a wattle. Although nominally a barber, Mr. Rentz constantly roams Northern Ontario in search of gold, a pursuit at which he is moderately successful. While prospecting he finds natural objects such as tree burls, root formations and branches that suggest certain sculptural forms to him. These he brings home and stacks behind his workroom, in sheds and outdoors until he has time to coax out the forms with paint, the addition of limbs in some pieces, and the liberal use of plastic wood. Some of Mr. Rentz's creations are distinctly impressionistic, only suggesting a certain form, while others display a sharp sense of the whimsical and humorous.

183.
Bellhop
Ewald Rentz, Beardmore,
Ontario
ca. 1975
Painted wood
49 x 31 x 16 cm
CCFCS 80-118

The basis for the comical monkey bellhop is a branch formation found by Ewald Rentz on one of his many gold-prospecting trips in Northern Ontario. With the addition of shoes, a hat, and the two suitcases with their humorous signs, the piece is a splendid combination of wit and what the artist calls "completed" art.

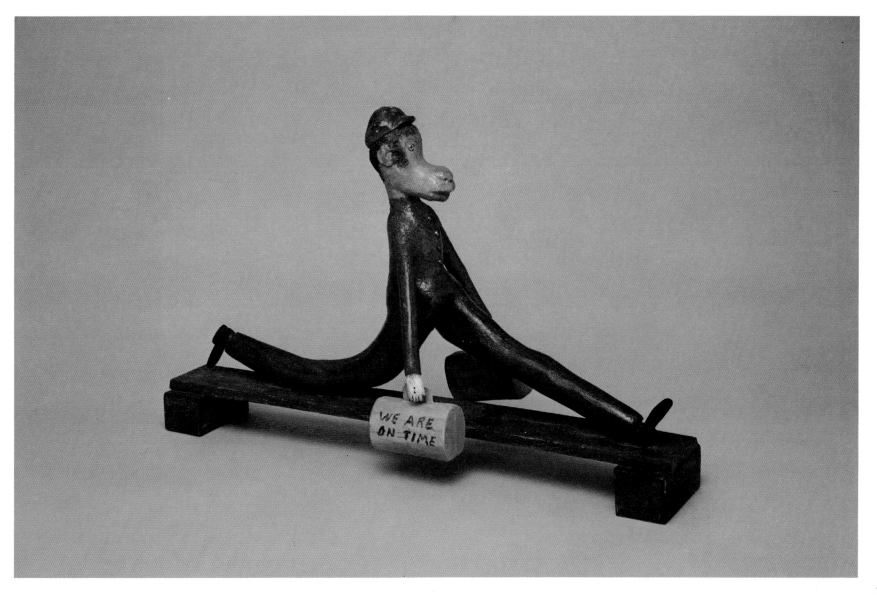

184.

The Cold Lumberjack

Yvonne Bolduc, Baie-Saint-Paul, Québec
Twentieth century
Painted wood
16.5 x 6.5 x 2 cm
CCFCS 74–201

Yvonne Bolduc is better known as a painter in the folk tradition, and some of her early carvings have only recently come to light. The daughter of a carpenter, she spent much of her childhood in her father's shop, absorbing and practising the art of woodworking. When the nearby highway was diverted to run right past the shop, the Bolduc family found that there was a market for small, inexpensive carvings, both in relief and freestanding. Since 1923, Miss Bolduc has created a large number of these figures, often modelled on well-known radio characters who are readily recognizable to her customers. Women carvers are very rare in Canada, making this an unusual piece in that sense, but the masterful and humorous execution of the perpetually chilly lumberjack make it an outstanding work on its own merit.

185.
Notary Walking His Dog
Oscar Héon,
Cap-de-la-Madeleine, Québec
Mid-twentieth century
Painted wood
34 x 20 x 14.5 cm
Price Coll., CCFCS 79-1841

186.
Morning Exercise
Oscar Héon,
Cap-de-la-Madeleine, Québec
Mid-twentieth century
Painted wood
22 x 16.5 x 13 cm
Sharpe Coll., CCFCS 77-973

Although Oscar Héon had carved periodically from the time of his youth, carving became the primary occupation of the last years of his life. Using old fence posts or whatever softwood was available, he created mechanical toys, religious figures, and carvings that captured special moments of human experience. *Morning Exercise* was inspired by young mothers on a morning television programme. In the substantial and erect bearing of the notary with his dog, Mr. Héon portrays the self-satisfaction and prosperous air of a well-known village personality.

187.
"Haying in Manitoba, 1900"
Arthur L. Flett, Winnipeg, Manitoba
Mid-twentieth century
Painted wood, electric wiring,
fabric, leather, wire
51 x 51 x 27 cm
CCFCS 79-341

Arthur Flett has made several lamps, using as his materials "whatever is lying around". This piece, with the title *"Haying in Manitoba, 1900"* painted on it, may have been inspired by the artist's background; he was born in that year on a small farm outside Winnipeg. The couple in bathing suits are a favourite subject, dating from a time when he carved similar figures riding in a sleigh and presented them to visitors from Florida. Mr. Flett adds, convincingly, "No one had ever seen anything like it before."

188.
Carved Chain
Richard Young,
Grenville, Québec
1980
Wood
63 x 2.5 x 2.5 cm
CCFCS 81-348

Carving complex, free-moving objects from a single piece of wood is a long-standing tradition in many cultures. Carved chains were used in the Middle Ages as belts for the flowing robes of the period. Many other examples of complex carving, especially balls in cages (or "lanterns"), were completed by whittlers, sailors and prisoners as love tokens or mementoes.

Richard Young, the Québec carver of this complicated basswood piece, has been carving since 1933, and as his skill developed, has attempted to make each piece more intricate than the last. In this chain, two lanterns are held together by eleven links and a swivel.

The larger lantern contains an open cylinder and three balls, and is signed by the carver. The outsides of both lanterns are chip-carved, and the butt of the larger is adorned with a maple leaf. When asked why he made the piece so complex, he answered simply, "Because it's harder to do."

Dancing Dolls

(Numbers 189–195)

The tradition of articulated wooden dolls is well known throughout the Western world, and reached its peak with the so-called Dutch dolls, or "penny woodens", of the nineteenth century. In Canada, this type of doll is often crafted to dance in time to traditional music. Manipulated by a stick attached to its back, the loose-jointed doll is held above a flexible board, its feet lightly touching; the board is tapped in time to the music, causing the doll to bounce in noisy imitation of step or clog dancing.

The forms of these dancing dolls, or "limberjacks" as they are also known, vary considerably, some having articulated feet, arms and heads, in addition to the more commonly jointed knees and hips. Some are highly decorated and carved in three-dimensional form, while others are more simply made and are essentially flat. The dolls can also serve as outlets for the artist's sense of humour or whimsy, as is the case with the go-go dancer and the fisherman holding the jointed fish.

189.
Go-Go Dancing Doll
Eastern Canada
1960s (?)
Painted wood, fabric, hair
45.5 x 45 x 13 cm
CCFCS 77-152

This go-go dancer is more elaborate in movement, dress and comical detail than the traditional limberjack. Not only are the limbs articulated, but the breasts are also jointed, the head is bewigged with human hair, and the figure is suspended from a highly decorated frame.

190.
*Button-eyed
Dancing Doll*
Québec
Early twentieth century
Wood, ceramic
53 x 33.5 x 12 cm
CCFCS 76-170

Although somewhat less highly finished than the other dolls here, this specimen still displays a few decorative features, such as button eyes, a carved nose, and traces of painted red trousers. Wooden dowelling flexes the leg joints, while nails allow the arm joints to bend.

191.
Black Dancing Doll
Nova Scotia
Nineteenth century
Painted wood
36 x 9.5 x 7 cm
CCFCS 81-373

An example of the blackface dancing dolls, or limberjacks, of Nova Scotia, this well-aged specimen from the South Shore was probably made in the nineteenth century.

192.
Fisherman Limberjack
Ernie Canning,
Muskoka District, Ontario
1978
Painted wood
37 x 23 x 12 cm
CCFCS 78-260

193.
Lumberjack Limberjack
Ernie Canning,
Muskoka District, Ontario
1978
Painted wood
41 x 27 x 11 cm
CCFCS 78-262

The two Canning limberjacks are a departure from the traditional dancing-doll form. The limbs are joined with metal screw-eyes, which are not suitable for limberjack movement, but are nevertheless well suited for comical effects when the figure is bounced at the end of the holding-stick.

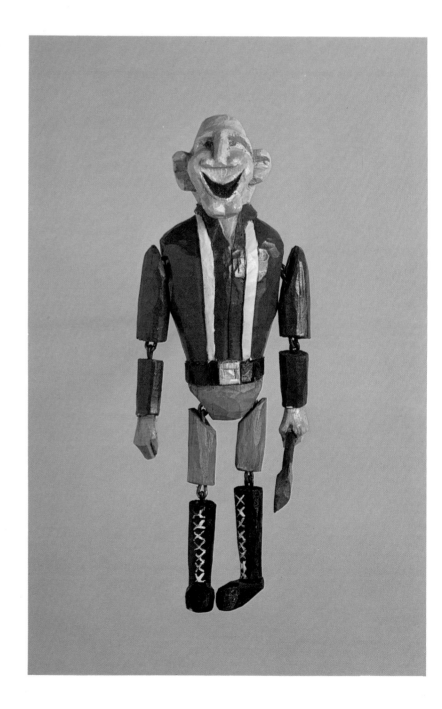

194.
*Formal
Dancing Doll*
Eastern Canada
Early twentieth
century
Painted wood
33.5 x 7.5 x 5.5 cm
CCFCS 82-138

This dancing doll displays considerable dignity, with his tailcoat and centre-parted hair. Originally designed for a dancing-stick, the figure is now suspended by a string, indicating that his dancing days may be over.

195.
Dancing Soldier
Toronto, Ontario
Twentieth century
Painted wood, metal, rubber tube, leather, fabric
79 x 17 x 13.5 cm
CCFCS 77-449

Although this limberjack-style doll cannot dance in the expected manner owing to his lack of knee joints, he can hold a cigarette in his mouth, which the operator smokes through a rubber tube. The figure has leather hands, boots and puttees, and medals made from military coat-buttons.

196.
"Catfish"
Gordon Murphy, Blandford,
Nova Scotia
ca. 1950
Painted wood, metal
20.5 x 13.5 x 7 cm
CCFCS 81-88

"Catfish" is a name attached to a wide variety of fish from both fresh and salt water. However, this specimen displays few of the common characteristics of the species, indicating that it may be the artist's unique conception of a catfish. The open mouth and the sharp teeth seem more reminiscent of a piranha.

197.
Peacock
Québec
ca. 1900
Painted wood
and thread
69 x 49 x 19 cm
CCFCS 81-66

Birds with fanlike tails and wings are part of a long-standing whittling tradition. Carved from a single block of straight-grained wood, the fan is carefully split, soaked for pliability and allowed to dry while spread.

This large example from Québec, made at the turn of the century, has thirty-five individual feathers, each carefully glued and tied with thread to its companion. As the figure is a peacock, each feather is painted with the feather's "eye", which had superstitious beliefs connected with it in many cultures.

198.
"The Holy Book"
George Hard, Toronto, Ontario
ca. 1920
Wood
28 x 20 x 4 cm
CCFCS 81-4

Boxes in the shape of a book have been an element in the carving tradition for centuries. They range from tiny containers for snuff, tobacco or spruce gum to larger boxes to hold bibles or missals. This specimen incorporates another traditional element—the enclosed snake that pops out when the front edge is slid open. Trick boxes operating on the same principle as this one have been known since the seventeenth century. Made by English-born George Hard, a longtime employee of the Canadian National Railways, the snake displays more intricate carving than the box itself. Mr. Hard carved for only a decade, having taken it up after retirement.

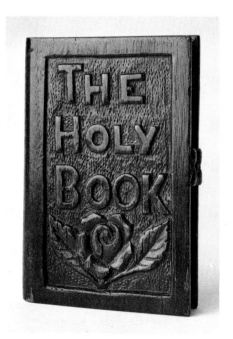

199.
Boy with Watermelon and Rabbit
Buttonville, Ontario
ca. 1920
Painted wood
78 x 44 x 35 cm
CCFCS 74-216

Related to a long-standing tradition in the United States, this lawn ornament is reminiscent of the cast-iron jockey and groom hitching-posts so common until a generation ago. The maker of this piece is thought to have been an itinerant carver who travelled through Ontario in the 1920s, selling his wares door to door. The racist overtones of the piece are clearly stated, and are reinforced by the slice of watermelon and the rabbit.

200.
Baptiste and the Three Pigs
Noé J. Champagne ("Ti-père artisse"),
Bishopton, Québec
1980
Synthetic rags on jute cloth
74 x 43 cm
CCFCS 80-482

A vitriolic criticism of Québec unions, this piece was created by the artist after being refused medical care during a strike of hospital staff. He feels that the only concern of the Corporation des syndicats nationaux (CSN), the Fédération des travailleurs du Québec (FTQ), and the Corporation des enseignants du Québec (CEQ rather than SEQ) for the Québec people, represented here by "Baptiste", is to feed off them. The colours of the pigs represent the physical appearance and ideological leanings of the union leaders: red for the CSN, pink for the FTQ, and yellow for the CEQ.

201.
Mackerel Plough
Nova Scotia
ca. 1900
Wood, metal
17 x 5.5 x 2.5 cm
CCFCS 79-809

This small knife is of a type that may have been used to slit the sides of lean mackerel. The blade was fashioned from a copper penny, and the skilful carving of the handle makes it not only a functional tool, but also a constant reminder of the pleasures of life on shore.

202.
Spool Holder/Pincushion
Charlie Atkinson,
South Side, Cape Sable Island,
Nova Scotia
ca. 1970
Painted wood and metal, fabric
40 x 20.5 x 5 cm
CCFCS 77-294

Charlie Atkinson's wood carvings range
from the small models and decoys he
carved as a boy to the full-sized speed-
boats and lobster boats he built later.
As he grew older, he carved yard
ornaments and birdhouses, each made
"all fancy" with a coat of painted spots.
Most were sold over the fence to
passers-by. The strange conception of a
human face as a pincushion contrasts
with the gentle appeal of most of his
other work.

203.
"Hindou Goddess"
Ann Harbuz
North Battleford, Saskatchewan
1978
Painted beeswax, paintbrushes
75 x 50 x 25 cm
CCFCS 82-137

Accustomed to keeping busy with a
variety of arts and crafts, Ann Harbuz
showed little hesitation in trying
painting. That was in 1967, and since
then her scenes of pioneer life on the
Prairies, painted in various media, have
become well known in Canada. She
initially found a use for her
accumulated used brushes in a collage
in the shape of a butterfly. Later she
combined paintbrushes with a big piece
of beeswax to produce this more
unusual creation.

204.
Music Box
Alphonse Grenier,
Saint-Jean-de-la-Lande,
Beauce County, Québec
ca. 1970
Painted wood, glass, leather,
electric wiring, string
142 x 95 x 46 cm
CCFCS 79-436

Alphonse Grenier's skills as farmer,
mechanic, carpenter and inventor were
combined in the creation of this huge
music box. Its fifty characters are
activated by a complex system of pulleys
attached to an electric motor. The
bottom shelf contains the turntable on
which dance music is played as well as
carvings of a farmer and his chickens.
The shelf above shows the method of
processing flax, which both Grenier and
his wife were familiar with through
personal experience. The second shelf
contains scenes of Hell, a sharp contrast
with the happy gathering of people
playing music and dancing on the top
shelf. Grenier laughed off a suggestion
that he take out a patent on this device,
confident that only a "madman like me"
could duplicate the strange creation.

Comic Fantasies

(Numbers 205–207)

With time on his hands and an urge to decorate his yard, Collins Eisenhauer began carving in 1964. Most of his early creations were fairly large, but he soon began to carve small figures as well. These he liked to do because they did not "take much wood", and they enabled him to "keep quiet and do it just with my hands and brain". His small figures cover a wide range of subjects, including some odd relationships between humans and animals as well as nudes in a variety of situations. Many combine humour and a touch of the bizarre.

205.
Accordion Player and Dancing Cats
Collins Eisenhauer,
Union Square, Nova Scotia
ca. 1970
Painted wood
22 x 21.5 x 17 cm
CCFCS 77-271

206.
Woman Feeding Skunk
Collins Eisenhauer,
Union Square, Nova Scotia
ca. 1970
Painted wood
27 x 10 x 9 cm
CCFCS 77-286

207.
Bathroom Accident
Collins Eisenhauer,
Union Square, Nova Scotia
ca. 1970
Painted wood
34.5 x 19.5 x 17.5 cm
CCFCS 77-285

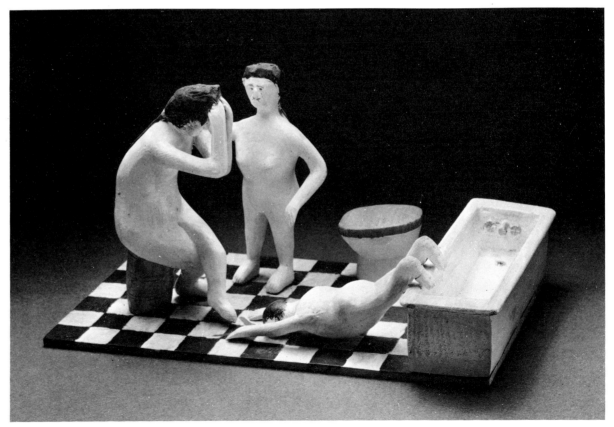

208.
Bird Tree
Waldorf Latoske, Winnipeg, Manitoba
ca. 1910
Painted wood, wire, cord
68.5 x 29 x 23 cm
CCFCS 75-7

A longtime favourite in the whittler's repertoire has been the bird tree, in which carved and painted birds are suspended from a central column in much the same way as in a modern mobile. Made by Waldorf Latoske, a Northern-European immigrant who came to Canada early in this century, this tree originally stood on a table made by the carver especially for the purpose. Perhaps it represents a world where a variety of species can live together in harmony. In Mr. Latoske's vision, the tiny cat seems to have little chance of disrupting this Eden.

209.
Hunting Satire
Adélard Turgeon,
Saint-Anselme, Québec
ca. 1950
Painted wood
70 x 54 x 43 cm
CCFCS 78-362

Adélard Turgeon was born in 1883 on his father's farm. He was apprenticed to the village blacksmith in his youth.

When he married he took over the family farm from his father and ran it until his retirement. Like most of the farmers at that time, Mr. Turgeon made almost everything needed on the farm himself. He made shoes for his family for many years. Adept at whittling, he spent his leisure time carving crucifixes, domestic and wild animals, and miniatures representing farms of the past. One of his works, a turkey, even won a prize at the Québec fair in the

1940s. According to one of his daughters, his carvings were made only for members of the family and to delight the children. "At that time, we never thought they would sell."

This scene, made of pine and apple-tree branches, of which there are at least two other versions, satirizes hunting. The hunter, his gun at the ready, is unaware of all the animals around him. As a point of interest, the Turgeon family has never eaten game.

210.
Painted Table
Joseph Norris,
Lower Prospect, Nova Scotia
1976
Painted wood
79 x 61 x 35 cm
CCFCS 77-310

Joe Norris's work is mainly easel painting, which he hangs in front of his house to sell. Occasionally, he paints his familiar scenes on furniture as well. "Looks different, though, to see something painted like that," the artist says. "People come down here really like it."

211.
Covered Chair
Albert Lohnes, West Berlin, Nova Scotia
ca. 1970
Wood, wool
93.5 x 51 x 45.5 cm
CCFCS 77-304

Over forty years ago, a ship's captain complained of sliding around in his chair during rough weather. Albert Lohnes was a member of the ship's crew, and he tells of solving the problem by knotting a non-skid cover for it. Mr. Lohnes had gone to sea at the age of thirteen and learned knitting and knotting while working in the net lofts. In semi-retirement ten years ago, he decided to try making chair-covers again. When it came to selecting colours, he used "whatever came to mind". The design of this cover includes the maker's name and a portrait of one of the ships he knew so well.

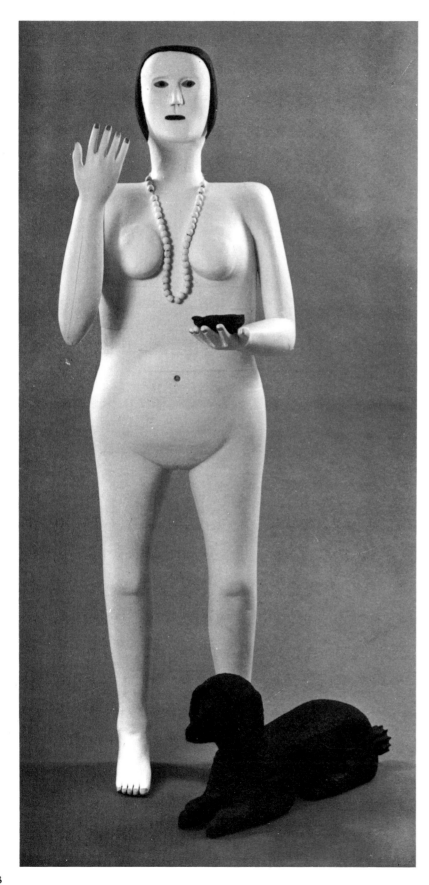

212.
"Penelope" and the Poodle
Clarence Moores,
Milton, Queens County, Nova Scotia
1976
Painted wood
Penelope: 161.5 x 54 x 53 cm
Poodle: 70 x 30 x 16 cm
CCFCS 77-373(1, 2)

While unemployed after a local mill shut down, Clarence Moores began carving a life-sized figure simply to pass the time. He had carved crooked-knife handles as a young man, and worked as a carpenter, but *"Penelope"* was his first attempt at making something so large. The main figure was cut from dozens of horizontally laminated planks; it was roughed out with a chain saw, trimmed with a hammer and chisel, and then sanded by hand. According to Moores, "I started to make a man and it changed into a woman." *"Penelope"* is in fact an ashtray holder, her smooth white surface contrasting strikingly with the rough texture of the black poodle.

213.
The World
Joe Sleep, Halifax, Nova Scotia
ca. 1970
Paint and ink on hardboard
182.5 x 122.5 x 0.5 cm
CCFCS 77-300

While in hospital in 1973, Joe Sleep took the brush and paints offered by the nurses, just to "keep out of trouble". Soon this jack-of-all-trades found that he had discovered a new way of making a living. The distinctive colours and stenciled shapes in his paintings owe something to the twenty-one years he spent working in a carnival touring the Maritimes. In this work the eye is held by the overall plan and arrangement of a personal fantasy of sky, earth and sea. Mr. Sleep painted for the market, producing as many as five hundred pictures in one year, many of which he sold personally in a public park. He was aware of which sizes and designs were most popular, but says he always relied on his "own judgement and ideas".

214.
Hall Coatrack
Eli Croft, Camperdown, Nova Scotia
Early twentieth century
Painted wood and antler, glass
229 x 137 x 66 cm
CCFCS 79-325

Working as a prospector and blacksmith, Eli Croft made his home in various towns of Lunenburg County during the years spanning the turn of the century. The range of his woodworking included knife handles, canes and furniture, and judging from the pieces that survived he was an excellent craftsman. Using wood, bone and antler, Mr. Croft developed a personal and highly decorative style in which portrayals of birds and animals combine with geometric motifs.

215.
Giraffe
Alcide Saint-Germain,
Saint-Antoine-Abbé, Québec
ca. 1971
Painted wood, plaster, plastic
220 x 190 x 90 cm
CCFCS 76-171

Inspired by a television lamp in the shape of a moose, Alcide Saint-Germain's first carvings were a series of moose for his garden and yard, one of which weighed over 600 kilograms. His tireless imagination also inspired him to create fanciful sculptures of animals not native to his region—penguins, giraffes and tigers, the last two exhibiting similar decorative motifs of circles, ellipses and white spots. Mr. Saint-Germain also created a series of jointed human figures, some of which could be controlled from inside the house to wave at passing motorists "to make them laugh"; others he took with him in the passenger seat of his car. A prolific carver, he successfully created his own natural environment on his front lawn, working principally in wood, which he covered with a thick coat of plaster and then painted.

216.
Duck Whirligig
Kost Pawlyk, Elk Point, Alberta
1980
Painted wood, metal
52 x 50 x 28 cm
CCFCS 81-236

Mechanically, this garden ornament is quite sophisticated. From its copper bushings to the well-balanced pairs of propellers on each side, the whirligig is capable of motion in the lightest of breezes. Mr. Pawlyk, an Albertan of Ukrainian background, decorated the piece in colours and geometric forms that suggest Hutsulian designs, a tradition from the Western Ukraine.

217.
The Chase
Gilbert Plains, Manitoba
Twentieth century
Painted wood and wire, metal
75 x 61 (diam.) cm
CCFCS 70-60

The chase scene is a well-known motif for whirligigs with a circular motion, such as this one with its bicycle-shaft axle. Four vertically hung cups, made from the same metal as the roof, catch the wind and give the piece the appearance of a tiny carousel.

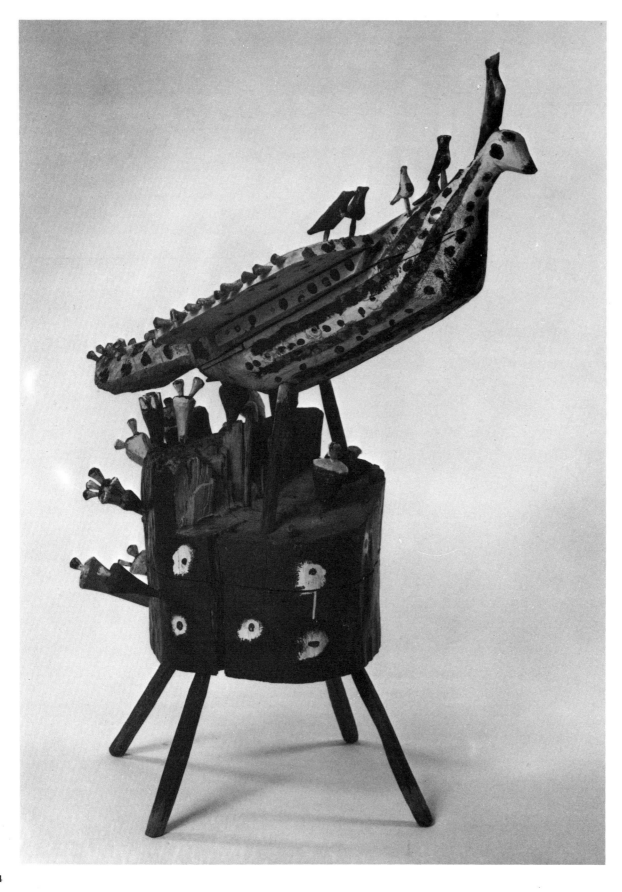

218.
Mother Bird
Edmond Châtigny,
Saint-Isidore, Dorchester County,
Québec
ca. 1975
Painted wood
121.5 x 95 x 61.5 cm
Price Coll., CCFCS 81-424

Perhaps because he has retired from his
farm to a house in the suburbs,
Edmond Châtigny has created in wood
a whole natural world in his front yard,
consisting of flowers, trees, shrubs,
birdhouses, birds, a penguin and other
small animals. Painted mainly with
green, pink, white and brown, Mr.
Châtigny's lively creations connect him
with the Québec *patenteux*, or yard-art,
phenomenon. Mother Bird, her
apparent offspring perched on her
wings and head, stands in a veritable
forest of flowers made from whittled
cedar plugs, each painted in several
colours.

219.
The Lantern Bearer
Arthur Erwin, Winchester, Ontario
1977
Painted wood, kerosene lamp
124 x 50 x 42 cm
CCFCS 80-401(1, 2)

Arthur Erwin began carving in 1969, a
very few years before his retirement.
After laminating pine boards together,
he carves his figures out with a saw and
a chisel. Starting with smaller pieces,
such as dogs, geese and ducks, Mr.
Erwin later began carving larger pieces,
including "four or five men", several
moose, and a totem pole for the front
yard. Reminiscent of the hitching posts
of a past age, *The Lantern Bearer* was
intended to light the path to the front
door. Unfortunately, the artist said, the
wind not only put out the lantern, but
caused it to swing against the figure,
damaging the paint.

Birdhouses

(Numbers 220–223)

Birdhouses are made for a variety of reasons. In addition to a safe nesting spot for birds, the makers of birdhouses variously view them as purely decorative garden ornaments, a means of recreating a specific memory—whether of a house, barn, grain elevator or architectural style—or simply as an outlet for the imagination.

Four different styles of birdhouses are presented here, including the Nova Scotian spotted house with its carved decoy birds, and the red and green barn with two weather-vanes, which is a delightful contrast to the large red, white and blue house with its cupola and dormers. *"Fernando's"*, though crude in actual construction, displays the whimsical imagination of its makers, with its sardine-can doorstep, bobbypin handrail, and delightful wall-paintings of an overflowing garbage can and an out-of-control lawn.

220.
Spotted Birdhouse
Charlie Atkinson,
South Side, Cape Sable Island,
Nova Scotia
ca. 1970
Painted wood
56 x 36 x 30 cm
CCFCS 75-907

221.
"Fernando's"
Schoolboys, Norway House, Manitoba
ca. 1970
Painted wood, metal
27 x 18 x 15 cm
CCFCS 70-203

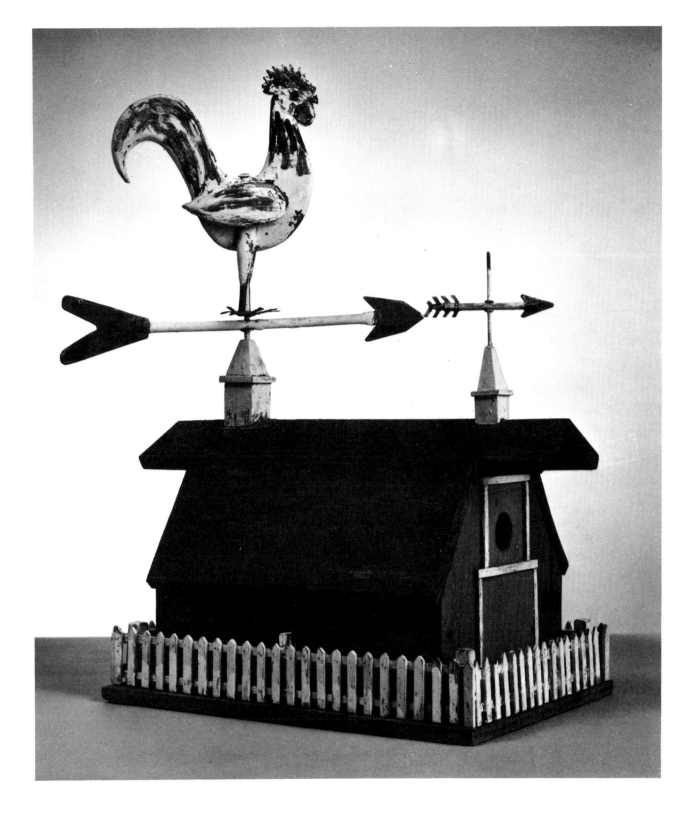

222.
*Red, White
and Blue Birdhouse*
William G. Loney,
Prince Edward County, Ontario
Mid-twentieth century
Painted wood and tin
94 x 82 x 72 cm
CCFCS 80-83

223.
Barn Birdhouse
John Ritcey, Lunenburg,
Nova Scotia
Mid-twentieth century
Painted wood and tin
60 x 55 x 29 cm
CCFCS 78-486

224.
Mountie
Carleton County, Ontario
Mid-twentieth century
Painted wood and metal
135 x 37 x 35.5 cm
CCFCS 78-437

Canada's most common national
symbols are beavers, maple leaves and
Mounties. Certain occupations have
become stylized expressions of
admiration in the folk vocabulary,
including the cowboy, the settler and
the sailor, but few are more popular
than the Mountie. As a lawn decoration,
this slender figure, with his pot-lid hat
and epaulets of corrugated fasteners,
personified the strength, honour and
devotion to duty attributed to those
legendary figures.

225.
Mailbox Cowboy
Ross W. Gould, Duntroon, Ontario
1970
Painted wood and metal, wire
90 x 59 x 49 cm
CCFCS 77-438

Distinctive mailboxes have long been a
standard feature of Canadian garden art.
Welded chain-link posts and ingenious
mechanical systems enabling the
mailbox to be raised above snowdrifts
are well-known features of this genre.
Unusual decorations on ordinary
commercial mailboxes are also relatively
common, this example showing a flair
for comic artistry. The lasso, cowboy hat
and colourful bandanna, the revolver
and the inevitable cigarette all
contribute to the traditional image of the
cowboy. This figure also holds a sign
proclaiming the name of his owner and
maker.

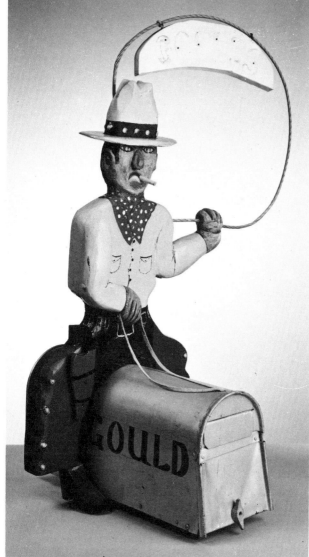

226.
Cowboy Whirligig
Leo Morton, Barss Corner, Nova Scotia
Twentieth century
Wood, metal
85.5 x 37 x 12 cm
CCFCS 77-307

Whirligigs of great variety dot the Canadian landscape. Common motifs include flying birds, sawyers and choppers, chase scenes, geometrically decorated plastic bottles, and every conceivable type of airplane. Although the history of this piece has been lost, we can still enjoy such delightful touches as the sombrero-hatted cowboy, the carving of his arms and the reins he holds from a single piece of wood, and the triumphant smile of the central figure.

227.
Horse and Rider
J. Seton Tompkins,
Singhampton, Ontario
1978
Painted wood, cord
126 x 123 x 24.5 cm
CCFCS 81-425

J. Seton Tompkins owned and operated a gas station for many years, and is reported to have said that the glossy finish on his sculptures resembles the shiny surface of the automobiles that were so much a part of his life. Although his earlier pieces tended to be somewhat static, this figure is more animated. The carving was originally intended to commemorate an Orange Day parade.

228.
Seated Woman
Québec
Twentieth century
Painted wood
135 x 66 x 53 cm
CCFCS 78-190

Many Québec carvers and decorators of the outdoor environment customarily placed one or more figures on their front porch. This figure of a seated woman, although unarticulated, would have looked enough like a real person to catch the notice of passers-by. Holding her cane and peering at the world with a fixed stare, she evokes a by-gone generation.

229.
The Colonel
Collins Eisenhauer,
Union Square, Nova Scotia
1976
Painted wood, eyeglasses
176 x 50 x 45 cm
CCFCS 81-57

Collins Eisenhauer's first mailbox holder was a life-sized Royal Canadian Mounted Policeman. After selling that figure, Mr. Eisenhauer made this portrait of Colonel Sanders to perform the same job. He too was eventually sold, and another replacement, a second colonel, had to be carved.

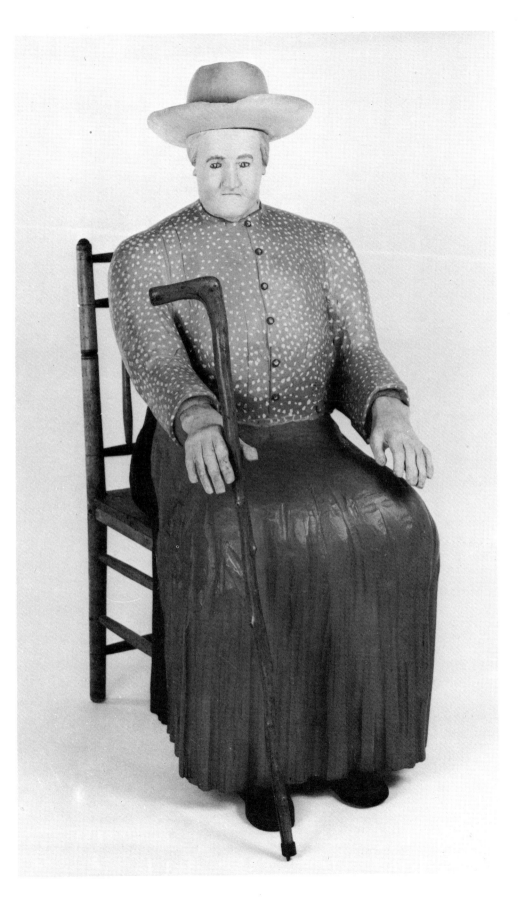

230.
Fiddler
Collins Eisenhauer,
Union Square, Nova Scotia
ca. 1975
Painted wood, wire, plastic
178 x 71 x 68 cm
CCFCS 77-282

A good many of Collins Eisenhauer's carvings were life-sized renditions of animals and humans, including portraits of Colonel Sanders, four politicians, and himself. The *Fiddler* was drawn from an experience he had at the South Shore Exhibition at Bridgewater, Nova Scotia, in about 1970. Mr. Eisenhauer saw a fiddler dressed in a red and white costume at a dance there, and determined to carve exactly what he had seen.

Politicians
(Numbers 231–232)

Collins Eisenhauer was among the first of the Maritime carvers to achieve national recognition as a folk artist. His carvings of four Canadian politicans—Pierre Elliott Trudeau, Robert Stanfield, David Lewis and Gerald Regan—first appeared in a parade in New Germany, Nova Scotia, in 1974 after a solid year of work. Despite the artist's allegedly serious approach to these subjects, the gesticulating Trudeau, with his plastic rose, and Stanfield holding the now-famous banana display the irrepressible Eisenhauer humour.

231.
Pierre Elliott Trudeau
Collins Eisenhauer,
Union Square, Nova Scotia
1974
Painted wood, metal, plastic, tar
133 x 65 x 50 cm
CCFCS 75-913

232.
Robert Stanfield
Collins Eisenhauer,
Union Square, Nova Scotia
1974
Painted wood, eyeglasses, metal, tar
146.5 x 57 x 48 cm
CCFCS 75-914

233.
Ti-Gus
Rosaire Leblanc,
Sainte-Sophie-de-Lévard, Québec
ca. 1960
Painted wood
88 x 37.5 x 35.5 cm
CCFCS 76-473

The traditional nickname for children in French Canada consists of the usual pet name combined with the prefix "Ti", a contraction of *petit*. Although "Gus" is not common, the comedy team of "Ti-Gus" and "Ti-Mousse" is very well known, making "Ti-Gus" an amusingly recognizable name, which may be why it became attached to this piece. It is probable that the curious truncated figure was a caricature of a diminutive man who lived in Leblanc's village. *Ti-Gus* originally stood on a tiny island in the carver's farm pond, a fantasy world Mr. Leblanc created to amuse his grandchildren. He was surrounded by other fanciful carvings, and had his own little house, into which he was moved each winter.

Four Artists

The final section of the exhibition focuses on four Canadian folk artists, whose works represent one or more of the major themes already developed. Nelphas Prévost adds decorative and symbolic details to everyday and "found" objects; Sam Spencer's carvings convey his love of nature and his own environment; the paintings of Frank Kocevar evoke the past but also express his commitment to his new home; and George Cockayne approaches the very limits of fantasy and imagination in his carvings. The artists represent the folk art of four provinces—Québec, Saskatchewan, British Columbia and Ontario—and employ a variety of techniques.

Although their works display great differences in style and execution, these four men share certain experiences and motivations that are expressed by the great majority of folk artists. None have had formal training, all have worked with their hands in a primarily rural setting, and each came to express his creativity relatively late in life. By examining the similarities and differences in these works, as well as the details and dynamics of the artists' lives and their attitudes toward art, we can begin to comprehend the vast complex of folk art in Canada.

Nelphas Prévost

b. 1904
Fassett, Québec

Nelphas Prévost was born on 7 May 1904 in Saint-André-Avellin, a village in Petite Nation, a former seigneury located in the Outaouais region of Québec, midway between Ottawa and Montréal. He spent his childhood on the family farm, where the work was hard and money was scarce. As farming and livestock raising provided barely enough to support a large family, the father worked in lumber camps to supplement the family's meagre income with the small wages he earned.

Nelphas learned the basics of farming at a tender age. Traditional society ignores adolescence; everyone has to work to meet the needs of the family; the children learn about both work and leisure by imitating the adults. Nelphas was introduced to various activities mainly by his older brother Abraham, who could fashion anything he wanted out of wood. Some members of the family also played the violin, and it was on the violin of his older brothers, who had left home to work, that Nelphas learned to "tame the instrument".

In his childhood Nelphas was attracted by nature, and he developed a taste for travel. He was soon working in lumber camps as a cook's assistant, then as a lumberjack and log driver in the forests of Québec and Ontario. There he encountered the rigours of nature and relentless bosses. The struggle started, not so much against nature and the forest as against bosses and foremen who abused their authority. He found in nature an inexhaustible source of solace and inspiration.

In 1930, Nelphas Prévost married Berthe Hayes, a childhood friend. The economic recession was in full swing and jobs were scarce, so the young couple lived with Berthe's parents. Nelphas looked after the farm work and the woodcutting. In the evenings they would play cards or dance. One evening, Mr. Hayes, who wanted a violin, asked Nelphas to make him one. After some hesitation, Nelphas set himself to the task and soon the Hayes family and friends were dancing to the strains of his instrument. His talent as a fiddler was soon recognized and admired throughout the seigneury.

A few years later, the Prévosts moved onto their own farm at Saint-André-Avellin. Nelphas found a permanent job at the mill in Brownsburg. He would spend his spare time whittling, his imagination set free by the shapes that emerged. He also continued to make violins, which he bartered for minor services. In 1970 he retired and began to spend most of his time making wooden tool-handles for his friends and acquaintances and carving for his own amusement.

Nelphas Prévost works in a woodshed near the house that he has turned into a workshop. His tools are simple—a hatchet, a few saws, a brace with several bits, a hammer and a sledgehammer, wood chisels, a pocketknife, a screwdriver with a flattened and sharpened end for use as a scraper, a couple of files, some sheets of glass, and sandpaper. He uses no mechanized or specialized tools. The work slowly takes shape under the adept and patient fingers of the artist.

The works of Nelphas Prévost that bear the most obvious imprint of nature are those he makes from driftwood, branches or roots whose natural forms suggest the subject to the artist, for example the bittern and the great anteater. Even when he carves more complicated works, such as his violin cases, the artist often retains the original form of the piece of wood. For example, the violin case decorated with a beaver on a fallen tree was carved from a single pine log, sawn lengthways and hollowed out to store the violin.

Making violins remains the artist's greatest challenge. Despite a limited range of tools, he is able to create remarkable precision instruments that are intricately decorated and bear witness to his limitless patience and uncommon dexterity. The ornamentation of the instrument is often of better quality than its sound. But, for the artist as well as his clients, these instruments are like icons—reminders of an era, a joie de vivre, and an aesthetic sense—as well as an indication of the artisan's undeniable mastery of the materials and techniques of his craft.

234.
Great Anteater
1979
Painted and varnished wood
95.5 x 37 x 36 cm
CCFCS 79-1567

Carved from a piece of driftwood, this animal of the tropics, feasting on ants, was seen by the artist on a television programme. The wood, flicked repeatedly with an electric drill, looks as though it were covered with ant holes. The piece is fastened to a foot with four toes, whose nails are painted red.

235.
Bittern
1980
Stained and varnished wood
131 x 82 x 31.5 cm
CCFCS 80-541

This stylized bird was made from
pieces of wood in whose natural forms
the artist saw the silhouette of a bird.

236.
White Ermine
1981
Painted and varnished wood
17.5 x 14.5 x 13.5 cm
CCFCS 81-336

The ermine emerges spontaneously from
the pine log, which retains its natural
appearance.

237.
Black Bear
1979
Painted and varnished wood
26 x 18.5 x 9.5 cm
CCFCS 79-1566

This simple sculpture conveys a
menacing yet controlled strength.

238.
Bull
1980–81
Painted wood
42.5 x 42 x 24.5 cm
CCFCS 81-341

The astrological sign of the artist is
Taurus, and his wife sometimes called
him "mon taureau" (my bull) because
of his robust physique—possibly
providing the inspiration for this
unusual hat rack.

239.
Violin Case
1968–79
Painted and varnished wood
84 x 24 x 15 cm
CCFCS 80-540.2

This violin case is shaped like a
snowshoe. Various natural and cultural
motifs are carved on the cover—a lynx
on a stump, fir trees, a well, a bow and
an arrow incorporating an "Indian's
finger". The sides of the case are made
of a single plank of wood curved under
pressure. Although started in 1968, this
piece was not carved and assembled
until 1978–79.

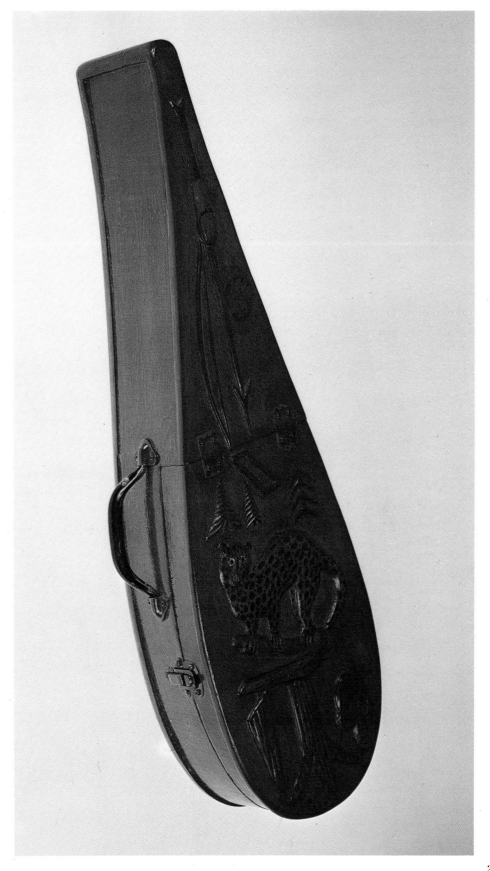

240.
Violin Case
1969–70
Painted and varnished wood
70 x 21.5 x 12 cm
CCFCS 80-546

This case for a small violin was made of a single pine log sawn in two lengthways and hollowed out. A beaver gnawing at a fallen spruce decorates the cover.

241.
Violin Case
1978
Painted and varnished wood
77.5 x 28 x 12 cm
CCFCS 79-1560.3

This violin case is made of spliced, incised strips of wood. The nailhead motif is repeated in several rows along the sides. The cover is decorated with six incised wheels painted red; the rims, spokes and hubs are black. According to the artist, they represent, from the largest to the smallest, a calèche wheel, a cart wheel, the large back wheel of a wagon, the small front wheel of a wagon, and the large back wheel and small front wheel of a buggy. The case is signed on the back, "1978/É.N.P. 74./S.A.N.S." (74 years old).

242.
Violin with Stars
1968
Painted and varnished wood
61.5 x 18.5 x 9.5 cm
CCFCS 79-1560.1

The sides of the body are made of
laminated strips of wood put together
with staggered joints. Four black stars
are painted on the soundboard, which
is of spruce. The back is made of maple
and is decorated with a maple leaf,
three stars and a blue spruce. The
soundboard and the back are outlined
with a black line. Mr. Prévost replaced
the traditional scroll with a cylinder,
whose ends form a rosette. "E.N.P.
1968" is inscribed on the inside of the
back and the initials "ENP" are on the
back of the fingerboard. Recalling his
youth, the artist confided: "Those were
the horse-and-buggy days! You would
put your violin under the seat of the
buggy and go to the party. When you
got there, the violin was a mess, the
strings loose. You just fixed it."

243.
Oak Violin
1978
Painted and varnished wood
62 x 19 x 9 cm
CCFCS 80-540.1

The body of this violin is made of
swamp white oak, as indicated by the
inscription on the inside of the back:
"Bois, che bleu/Faite a. la. main/par.
E.N. Prévost" (Wood, swamp white
oak/Handmade by E.N. Prévost). The
chin rest and the tailpiece are made of
linden and are flecked with black. A
decorative branch is engraved on the
tailpiece. The base of the neck bears the
inscription "1978".

244.
Nailhead-Motif Violin
1979–80
Stained and varnished wood
58.5 x 20 x 9.5 cm
CCFCS 80-547

Nelphas Prévost made this violin in the
winter of 1979–80 to demonstrate his
artistic capabilities. The sides and the
back of the body were carved from a
single pine log. The soundboard is also
of pine. The back and the soundboard
are outlined by the nailhead motif, and
a chain of nailheads crosses the back
lengthways. There is a bird's foot in
relief on the tailpiece. The chin rest, the
pegs and the fingerboard, which is
decorated with a plant and bears the
inscription "1980 ans", are made of
sumac. An alert beaver whose tail
merges with the maple neck of the violin
replaces the traditional scroll. The body
is stained dark brown and the edges
have been wiped to accentuate the relief.
The violin was completed in time to be
used at a fiddler's festival held in Pointe-
au-Chêne, Argenteuil County, in
July 1980.
   Since the body of the violin is of
softwood, the tone is weak. However,
Mr. Prévost himself admits that he is an
amateur instrument-maker, who is
noted more for his imagination than his
technical virtuosity; he seeks to create
an icon rather than a musical
instrument.

245.
Lion's-Head Violin
1981
Stained and varnished wood
60.5 x 19.5 x 9.5 cm
CCFCS 81-347

This violin was made in the summer of 1981 during the production of a television documentary illustrating Nelphas Prévost's technique. The sides and the back of the body were carved from a single plank of maple. The soundboard is made of linden. The neck, pegs and end-button are made of maple, whereas the fingerboard, the chin rest and the tailpiece are of sumac. A lion's head replaces the traditional scroll; it represents, for the artist, one of the animals on the Canadian coat of arms. The body is stained a mahogany colour and is covered with a clear varnish. The inside back bears the inscription: "Fait par Nelphas Prévost, le 20 août 1981" (Made by Nelphas Prévost, 20 August 1981).

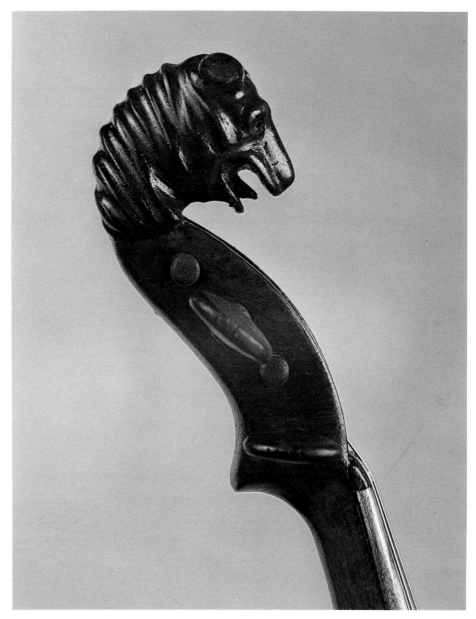

Sam Spencer

b. 1898
Saskatoon, Saskatchewan

"I started this picture business in 1927", chuckles Sam Spencer as he glances at the sixty-three relief carvings that cover his living-room walls. "It's just been a pastime, a hobby, you know, but it's hard work!...I do them for my own pleasure, not for sale."

Born in England in 1898, he was christened Arthur B. Spencer, but soon acquired the permanent nickname "Sam". Orphaned at the age of three, he settled on a homestead two years later near Punnichy, Saskatchewan, with an uncle and his paternal grandmother. There was no school for Sam to attend and there were few white children within visiting distance, so he worked on the farm and found a few friends on the Indian reserves nearby. At the age of eleven he began trapping for himself, but felt that his inability to read or write would prevent him from making "big money". So he taught himself to read the Bible and went on to prosper in the fur business and later in the construction boom in the United States.

Sam Spencer returned to the farm in 1924 and stayed there until 1941, when he and his aging uncle moved to Saskatoon. Even in the city he made every effort to be "as close to nature as possible". A huge garden and several pet squirrels became an important part of his life, and wildlife subjects predominated in his carvings. One positive feature of city life was the opportunity to socialize. Mr. Spencer never married, but in Saskatoon he befriended hundreds of children over the years. For a long time the highlight of his week was to take his young friends to the Saturday-afternoon movies.

Sam Spencer's art reflects his life and loves. He was an outdoorsman, a lover of nature, a loner, and yet a friend to all. His artistic subject-matter progressed from copied images to creative selections from his vivid memories. "I think that I have made better carvings from memories than from pictures", he says. Technically, he strove for ever-higher relief in his carvings, challenging the wood and himself. He discarded several pieces simply because his knife slipped: "Anything that's not in one piece, I do not want." His tools are simple—a pocketknife and a bent paring knife, "to get back in underneath there".

"Carving is like writing a book", the artist says. The carvings were done for his own enjoyment and Sam Spencer really does enjoy them, even the forty-year-old exploratory pieces. He sits serenely in his living-room surrounded by his "books"—his art—which are an affirmation of himself.

246.
Carved Frame
1926
Painted wood, photograph
51.5 x 47 x 3.5 cm
CCFCS 79-508

This frame is Sam Spencer's first attempt at jackknife artistry, and shows his own modification of the chip-carving technique that he learned from his English-born uncle. The photograph shows the artist on the homestead near Punnichy, Saskatchewan, with his favourite hunting dogs. Folk art is often an affirmation of self, and it is significant that this early creation served to accent, set apart, and perhaps mythologize Sam Spencer's self-image—an outdoorsman, close to nature in all its aspects.

247.
Letter-Rack
1927
Painted wood
34 x 27 x 8 cm
CCFCS 79-553

Sam Spencer's first attempt at "picture carving" was triggered by his grandmother's wish to have a favourite calendar illustration preserved. The horses' heads are carved in low relief on thin fruit-box boards. The chain was added in 1934 and the falcons around 1970, indicators not only of developing technique, but also of the artist's continuing interest in and regard for this personally meaningful early piece.

248.
Woman and Horse
1934
Painted wood
43.5 x 36.5 x 5 cm
CCFCS 79-505

This piece shows a distinct stage in the development of Sam Spencer's style and technique. While the image of the woman and horse was taken from a newspaper clipping, the frame is carved with his own selection of symbols and motifs from nature. It is an integral part of the total work, carved separately but attached to the centre block of wood. In later works Mr. Spencer would make a point of, and take pride in, carving his subject and frame from a single piece of wood.

249.
"The End of a Perfect Day"
1936
Painted wood
61 x 57.5 x 4.5 cm
CCFCS 79-516

Sam Spencer's love of nature and the outdoors began to be expressed more fully in his carvings in the mid-1930s. In this work the relief is higher than in his earlier pieces, and the subdued natural colours are well suited to the subject and the time of day. The board is of heavy 5-cm stock and is tapered, thicker at the bottom than at the top. The artist "never hunted for sport, only for meat."

THE. END. OF. A. PERFECT. DAY.

SAM. SPENCER. 1936.

250.
"There-ll-ways Be an England"
1939
Painted wood
38 x 28 x 4 cm
CCFCS 79-519

Its title taken from the patriotic song popular at the outbreak of the Second World War, this work was based on a photograph of the First World War regiment that Sam Spencer's uncle belonged to. Artists' ideas come from many sources, and are obviously modified to suit personal taste. This piece has been highly individualized in its translation from a two-dimensional source into a carved relief and by the addition of a foreground figure to suit Mr. Spencer's own artistic sense.

251.
Prairie Chicken
1942
Painted wood
16.5 x 10 x 4 cm
CCFCS 79-524

After retiring to the outskirts of Saskatoon in 1941, Sam Spencer had more time to carve, and he produced a series of affectionately rendered animal studies. This bird is carved in high relief, with the head, neck, legs and tail completely separated from the background.

252.
Pheasant
1945
Painted wood
51 x 28 x 4 cm
CCFCS 79-507

Sam Spencer's growing confidence in
his composition is evident in this piece.
The uncluttered, low-relief carved
background and frame contrast with the
dominant strength and colour of the
bird. The complexity of this piece
stands out in the artist's memory: "It's
about fifty colours on that."

253.
"War Dance"
1946
Painted wood
68.5 x 39 x 5.5 cm
CCFCS 79-520

Sam Spencer grew up near several Indian reserves and had many Indian friends, who invited him to dances and ceremonies. These memories and a newspaper photograph were the sources of this work. The intricate beadwork was painted with the tip of a needle held under a magnifying glass, and the frame was carved and painted in a distinctive and complementary design.

254.
Squirrel
1947
Painted wood
18 x 13 x 5.5 cm
CCFCS 79-534

Sam Spencer kept a number of pet
squirrels over the years, and this
carving, with its bulging lower body, "is
just the way they look in the fall". This
is the only piece with a cut-out
background in the collection. The frame
is tapered, narrower at the top than at
the bottom, allowing a better view of the
squirrel when the piece is viewed at an
angle.

255.
Moose
1947
Painted wood
38.5 x 26.5 x 5.5 cm
CCFCS 79-515

This magnificent animal has always been a popular subject for Canadian artists and photographers. Sam Spencer once saw a trophy moose-head in a hotel and "looked at it for almost a half hour", memorizing every detail. Years later he pulled the image from his memory bank and carved this piece. The relief is high, with the forward rack of horns well removed from the background. The distinctive pattern carved into the frame is somewhat reminiscent of elements in the woodwork of early-twentieth-century hotel lobbies and bars. The artist speaks fondly of this piece: "It looks so natural when it is in real light."

256.
Mountain Sheep
1950
Painted wood
35.5 x 26 x 5.5 cm
CCFCS 79-513

"If my knife had slipped on one of these corner heads I would have burned the whole piece." Sam Spencer's carving technique, his personal standards, goals and courage are all reflected in this work. He speaks of the ease of carving one corner head, but emphasizes the difficulty of matching three more to it.

257.
Eagle and Fish
ca. 1960
Painted wood
68 x 32 x 9.5 cm
CCFCS 79-552

This is Sam Spencer's favourite wildlife carving. "That's done by memory. I've seen eagles many times in different parts of the country. I just put the fish on there for his supper—you can always try and figure something up." The wing feathers are boldly carved, layered and painted, and the play of light on the glossy finish seems to give life to the piece.

258.
Angel and Child
1965
Painted wood
48.5 x 40 x 5 cm
CCFCS 79-512

Sam Spencer is a great friend of the
neighbourhood children, and the
memories in this piece are especially
meaningful to him. The angel's neck
and hair and the kneeling child are
modelled on the characteristics of some
of his young friends. The artist says he
has the ability to look at something for a
few minutes and then store the detailed
image in his mind for use at any time in
the future.

259.
Hockey Player
1978
Painted wood
29 x 23 x 4 cm
CCFCS 80-328

Sam Spencer listened to radio
broadcasts of National Hockey League
games when Charlie Connacher played
for the Toronto Maple Leafs. The small
player at the top is celebrating the Leafs'
winning the Stanley Cup. The goal-
like enclosure at the bottom depicts play
around the net, while an arrangement of
hockey sticks and pucks surrounds the
entire composition.

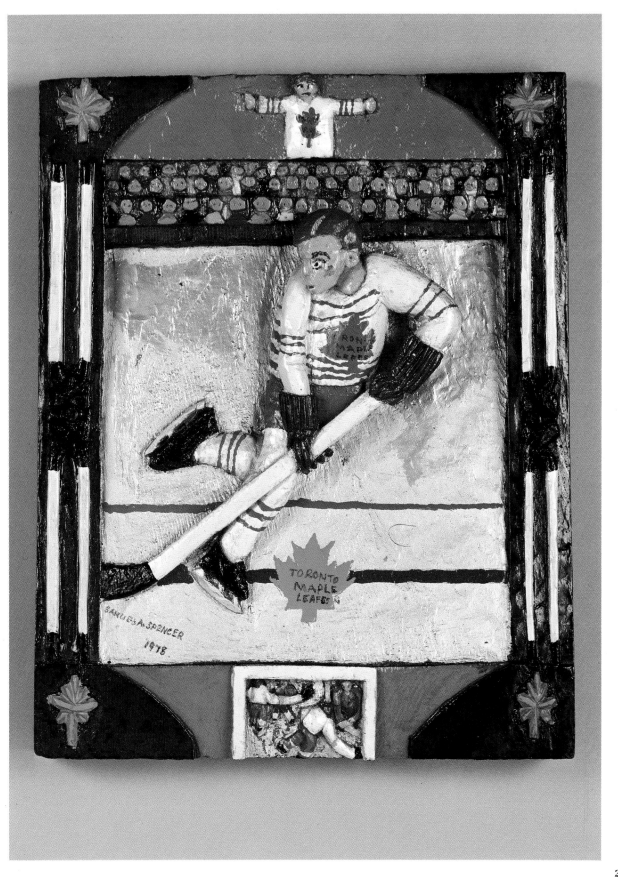

Frank Kocevar

1899–1982
Kelowna, British Columbia

Frank Kocevar enjoyed life in British Columbia's Okanagan Valley after his retirement in 1964, but, like so many immigrants of his generation, his memory pulled him back to his homeland, to the First World War, and to the early years of settling in a new country. His paintings, which became a way of passing time after a life of heavy labour, document this progress.

Mr. Kocevar started painting because he "didn't have anything else to do". The house and yard were fixed up and he felt at loose ends. During his active life no work had been too hard, and he felt that keeping busy was an essential part of proper living. At first it was very difficult because no one had ever shown him how to paint and he never asked. "So, I just practise till it's good. I'm my own critic. If it's no good I burn them." Although he never considered himself an artist, he quickly developed opinions and a set of standards for evaluating painting. The most important thing is "to know what it is". You've got to "have a motive". Frank Kocevar had a deep religious faith and strong beliefs about nationality and allegiances, and they became part of what he considered important in painting. He also felt that pictures "should be alive" with animals, birds, movement and the colours of spring.

Gradually people began visiting him to see his paintings. Some just looked for a few minutes, but many others stayed and asked Mr. Kocevar to paint for them. He had planned to capture larger and more elaborate scenes on his canvases and even to write about some of the events of his past. Yet, the paintings he finished form a vivid record of the impressions of a working man.

DONNALU WIGMORE

260.
"Tri Crshes Side by Side in Slovenia, Yugoslavia"
1964–79
Oil on hardboard
98 x 67.5 x 4 cm
CCFCS 79-413

When a Royal Canadian Mounted Policeman rode 65 kilometres over the Saskatchewan prairie to deliver induction orders from the Slovenian army, Frank Kocevar was torn between love of his homeland and his growing allegiance to Canada. Ultimately, he declined to serve again and decided to adopt his new home permanently.

He remembered his birthplace, however, as "a nice village, a nice church there. We got the job ringing bells; for eleven years we had that job. I rang bells so the people pray; you know, Angelus, at noon, in the evening, and at seven o'clock in the morning."

261.
"Lunch Time"
1964–79
Oil on hardboard
67 x 52 x 2.5 cm
CCFCS 79-396

This painting depicts a house in a Polish village that Frank Kocevar saw as a soldier during the First World War. While the troops moved through, he went "in to ask if I could buy... something, maybe buy some milk for ten cents or a piece of bread or a bun or something like that. I come in and ask, and she was nursing two kids.... There was a boy and a girl, one on each side, and there on the table was a lunch and the cat was in there, and the dog. They have a clock and they have a lamp hanging down. This is more elaborate than I saw. They got the nice cupboards and the nice dishes in there."

262.
Victory in Death
1964–79
Oil on hardboard
68.5 x 47.5 x 4 cm
CCFCS 79-402

As a soldier in the Austrian army during the First World War, Frank Kocevar developed a consuming hatred for war. "War is wrong," he said. "You have to kill to be a hero." Scenes from the war nonetheless became a recurring theme in his painting. Here we see "a mortally wounded sergeant, and he is praying like you see it, and Christ appear to him and tell him, 'You won.' That's a victory when you win and Christ told him he won.... He went to heaven."

263.
The Good Shepherd
1964–79
Oil on canvas
48 x 38 x 4 cm
CCFCS 79-397

Religion played a part in Frank Kocevar's life and painting. As he put it, "I can't ignore God. If I do, then I ignore everybody." This painting is of "a Good Shepherd. He holds the little sheep, you know. He is the Good Shepherd and the rest of them were around Him. That motif I got from a little card from Belgium. So I thought it was nice, so I paint one."

264.
"On the Willow Bunch Trail in 1870"
1964–79
Oil on hardboard
58 x 47.5 x 4.5 cm
CCFCS 79-398

Arriving in Canada from Slovenia in 1924, Frank Kocevar was sent to southern Saskatchewan to the small town of Willow Bunch. Using sign language, he managed to find a place to sleep and to buy some food. The next day he made his way to his first job, on a farm 10 kilometres away. It was also here that he met the woman who became his wife. The painting recalls the pioneer era in the place where his Canadian life began.

ON the WILLOW BUNCH TRAIL IN 1870.

Prairie Life

(Numbers 265–266)

The prairie snowscape made a strong impression on immigrant farmers from Europe. Frank Kocevar remembered driving teams of horses "ten or eight or four or two—you had to be good." The Plains Indians became a popular subject for his images of prairie life.

265.
Four-Horse Team
1964–79
Oil on wood
65 x 50 x 2 cm
CCFCS 79-418

266.
"Bringing News"
1964–79
Oil on hardboard
65 x 44.5 x 2 cm
CCFCS 79-399

In the Mines

(Numbers 267–268)

By 1936, drought, grasshoppers and the Depression had driven many farmers from the Prairies. Among them, Frank Kocevar and his wife moved to the mining town of Kimberley, British Columbia. There he managed to get work, and he spent the next twenty-seven years "underground". He said, "I never like it, the mine, not one day, but I was forced to do; that's the only thing I could get.... The outside sun, the blue sky, never look so good to you as when you come from the dark mine. That's the hard life."

267.
"Miner in Sulivan Mine 1940"
1964–79
Oil on canvas
34 x 26.5 x 2 cm
CCFCS 79-410

268.
*"Men Goin in the Mine
(Portal of Sulivan Mine)"*
1977
Oil on hardboard
70.5 x 55.5 x 5 cm
CCFCS 79-403

241

269.
"Pice River Contry"
1977
Oil on wood
67 x 46.5 x 2.5 cm
CCFCS 79-407

Frank Kocevar liked to see a painting complete and full of life. If there was a grain elevator there had to be a railway track and a town: "If it's empty, look like hell." Here the landscape cradles the settlement. "I like to see birds and thing like that; you could see a train going; all those are alive."

270.
"The Peaceful Valley"
1977
Oil on hardboard
67 x 46.5 x 2.5 cm
CCFCS 79-405

This painting brings together many of Frank Kocevar's ideas of how "things should look". For one who has faced hardship, struggle and isolation in a harsh environment, the "peaceful valley" with church, hospital and neighbours is a long-treasured dream.

George Cockayne

b. 1906
Madoc, Ontario

George Cockayne's carvings are at the margin of what is usually considered folk art; yet he shares with many little-known and untrained artists an awesome creative skill and imagination. Arriving in Canada as an orphan in the early 1920s, he has worked on farms and in lumber camps ever since. In the late thirties he had saved enough to buy a "rock-and-bush" farm in central Ontario, which remains his home.

For George Cockayne, art has been a way of preserving a long and well-developed relationship to the land while continuing to utilize its raw materials and engaging in the battle of wits and imagination necessary to make something of it. Through the activities associated with carving, he continues to shape the land, to demarcate it, to feel "in tune" with it.

Art has also been a way of preserving a relationship with the past, a last link with memories of youth, of neighbours now passed away, and of animals, such as the big black dog and his favourite farm animals. It "catches in your throat" to look at carvings that embody them now and they have become difficult for him to part with.

Through his art it has been possible for George Cockayne to maintain a link with the world beyond his own dirt road. His art has been a means of continuing to meet people, of getting some response to his ideas and of sharing his beliefs and problems.

Most crucial has been the role of his art in the preservation of a personal equilibrium, bringing a feeling of self-worth to a life that has often been lonely and difficult. What he has done of necessity and to "make a go of it" in everyday life, he continues to do in carving, that is, to use his imagination.

As he proclaims proudly, "People say I have the damndest mind you ever saw." About his recent work, most done with very limited sight, he continues: "Nobody else makes them. Why, I invented the damn silly things!...I guess I just do them my own way, and that's what puts the charm on 'em."

ERICA CLAUS

244

271.
"Sailor on Leave"
ca. 1930
Painted wood, nails
28 x 11 x 10 cm
CCFCS 75-1055

As a boy in England, George Cockayne lived near the sea and learned from a sailor how to whittle tiny boats. While working the central-Ontario lumber camps during the Depression, he recalled those days through this carving, one of his earliest still in existence.

272.
Shelf Bracket
ca. 1930
Painted wood
15.5 x 6.5 x 3 cm
CCFCS 75-1056

George Cockayne has always liked to use his spare time to recycle things that others threw away and to use his imagination to make something ordinary into something beautiful. His skill in carving female forms developed during long winters in the lumber camps. Finding his models in books and magazines, he tried to make them lifelike without being "too dirty". Although a bachelor all his life, he has appreciated the "female form divine; it always gets 'em, from the Eskimos down to Brazil."

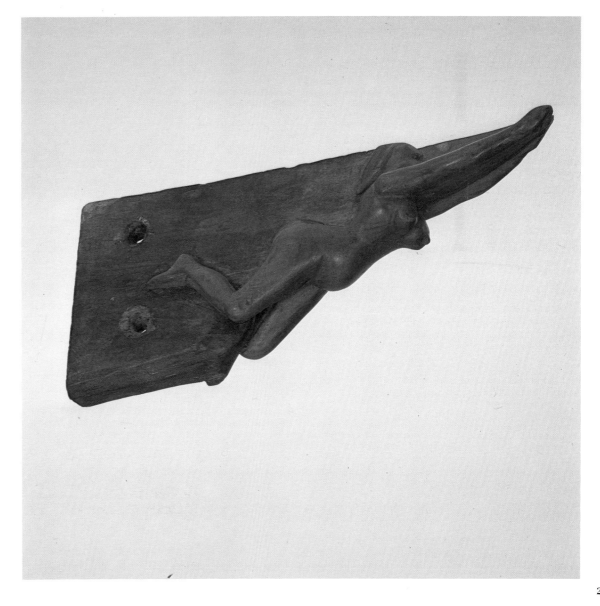

273.
"Peewee"
ca. 1930
Painted wood, shotgun shells
29.5 x 28 x 5 cm
Price Coll., CCFCS 79-1849

This carving was done while George Cockayne was a farmhand and logger, living on an island in the Bay of Quinte, Lake Ontario. He trained a ferret, which he named "Peewee", to assist him and his Great Dane to hunt rabbits, whose meat supplemented his meagre diet. As we see here, "When the ferret goes snooping around in the hole, the rabbit pops out." All the important details of this period of Mr. Cockayne's life are present in the composition—his dog, the ferret cage, his cabin and rowboat, and, surmounting the whole composition, his ferret.

274.
Doorstop Lady
1960
Painted wood, nails
163 x 31 x 23 cm
CCFCS 75-1057

According to George Cockayne, the doorstop was "the top of a cedar tree.... I'm making countless cedar fence posts and I wondered what I could do with that piece. I needed something to hold my door open.... That door catches an enormous amount of wind, and things have got to be tight." The doorstop was without a head for a year or two and then, because "it looked something like a woman", he made a head for it and painted the body. When you're a bachelor, "it's nice to have someone to come home to."

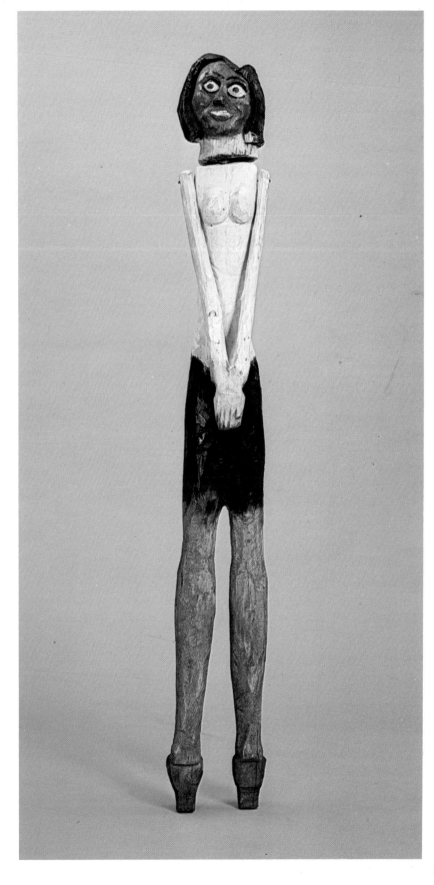

275.
Model Log Cabin
1970
Painted wood, rope, metal,
fabric, glass
72 x 58 x 46 cm
CCFCS 80-413(1–18)

The popular folktale about Red Riding Hood became the subject for this scene, built around a log cabin. Red Riding Hood stands with the Woodcutter, and the Wolf lies in the bed inside. Special care has been given to the details of construction and to the interior furnishings—the kind of care one would expect from a man who has himself built log cabins and lived in them. As usual, George Cockayne doesn't confine himself to just one story. The panel on the front of the cabin shows the carver's view of a backwoods election campaign, with canvassing being done with a club.

276.
Hard-Hat Holder
1970
Painted wood, putty, pins
41 x 27 x 21 cm
CCFCS 75-1053

For George Cockayne, a block of wood with a face carved on it was just "something to hang my hat on". A second face seemed to make sense, considering all the blank space on the back and how difficult it was to find a good piece of wood to carve. Around his farm, "nothing is wasted." The male face is the portrait of a neighbour.

When the neighbour's wife rejected Mr. Cockayne's offer of the carving, he carved a woman's face on the other side to show "what he thinks of women". Referring to the tongue, he says, "A lot of women will do that behind your back, lots of 'em."

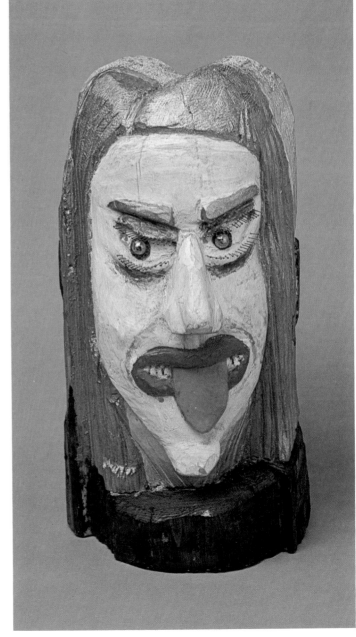

277.
"Beware the Yellow Band"
1975
Painted wood, nails
151 x 56 x 44 cm
Price Coll., CCFCS 79-1848

While pitching hay for his cows, George Cockayne came across "a wicked little snake, coiled up so it looked like the knitted handle of a woman's handbag." Later he read in a book that a snake with yellow bands could be dangerous, so he created the image that came to mind. He thought that it could stand in the foyer of a large house and the butler could place callers' cards on the tray. As with all his carvings, however, the interest was in making it rather than having it around. As he said, "That snake business, it stuck around. I damn near put it in for firewood more than once."

278.
"The Raja"
ca. 1975
Painted wood, pins, marbles, plastic
39 x 25.5 x 22.5 cm
Price Coll., CCFCS 79-1850

That every object should have its use is
very important to George Cockayne.
This bust, inspired by a picture in a
magazine, features a small opening
hollowed out of the back, with a door in
the shape of a bathtub. When closed it
appears as if two women are sitting in
the tub. A miniature version of the
"Yellow Band" sculpture is carved on
one side of the bust.

279.
"Omega"
1975
Painted wood, marbles, pins, string
58 x 39 x 37.5 cm
CCFCS 77-735

"Omega" repeats the interest in cannons and turtles evident in some of George Cockayne's other carvings. The artist, an avid reader before his eyesight failed, has maintained a perspective on world events through radio broadcasts. The slow movement of the Arab forces during the Six-Day War with Israel inspired this composition. *Omega*, the last letter of the Greek alphabet, symbolizes "the end". The slogan carved along the edge of the shell—"No matter where you are or what you do, there's always something wrong"—is one of Cockayne's favourites, a fatalist way of taking setbacks in stride.

Bibliography

American Folk Art: the Art of the Common Man in America, 1750–1900. 1932. Reprint. New York: Arno Press, 1969.

Ames, Kenneth L. Beyond Necessity: Art in the Folk Tradition. Winterthur, Del.: Winterthur Museum, 1977.

Amour et mariage: aspects de la vie populaire en Europe. Liège, Belgium: Musée de la vie wallonne, 1975.

Arts populaires du Québec. Québec: Musée du Québec, 1975.

Barbeau, Marius. "Les arts traditionnels". Pages 51–7 in La Renaissance campagnarde. Montréal: Albert Lévesque, 1935.

~ . Assomption Sash. National Museum of Canada, Bulletin 93. Ottawa: National Museum of Canada, [1937?]

~ ."The Field of European Folk-Lore in America". Journal of American Folklore 32 (124), 1919: 185–97.

~ ."Folk Arts in French Canada". Educational Record of the Province of Quebec, January–March 1942, pp. 40–5.

~ . Saintes artisanes, vol. 2, Mille petites adresses. Montréal: Fides, 1946.

~ ."Two Centuries of French-Canadian Wood Carving". Canadian Forum, March 1936, pp. 24–5.

~ ."Types de maisons canadiennes". Le Canada français, September 1941, pp. 35–43.

Barss, Peter. Older Ways: Traditional Nova Scotia Craftsmen. Toronto: Van Nostrand Reinhold, 1980.

Bird, Michael S. Ontario Fraktur: A Pennsylvania-German Folk Tradition in Early Canada. Toronto: Feheley, 1977.

Bird, Michael S., and Kobayashi, Terry. A Splendid Harvest: Germanic Folk and Decorative Arts in Canada. Scarborough, Ont.: Van Nostrand Reinhold, 1981.

Bishop, Robert Charles. American Folk Sculpture. New York: Dutton, 1974.

Blanchette, Jean-François. "Pour passer le temps, l'art folklorique. In L'art populaire au Québec, compiled by Jean Simard and René Bouchard. Montréal: Marcel Broquet, forthcoming.

Boas, Franz. Primitive Art. New ed. New York: Dover Publications, 1955.

Bonner, Mary Graham. Made in Canada. New York: Knopf, 1943.

Carufel, Hélène de. Le lin. Montréal: Leméac, 1980.

Christensen, Erwin O. Early American Wood Carving. 1952. Reprint. New York: Dover Publications, 1972.

~ . The Index of American Design. New York: Macmillan, 1950.

Crépeau, Pierre. "Mémoires en bois". In L'art populaire au Québec, compiled by Jean Simard and René Bouchard. Montréal: Marcel Broquet, forthcoming.

Crépeau, Pierre, and Blanchette, Jean-François. "Au-delà du sensible. La collection d'art populaire québécois au Centre canadien d'études sur la culture traditionnelle du Musée national de l'Homme, Ottawa." In L'art populaire au Québec, compiled by Jean Simard and René Bouchard. Montréal: Marcel Broquet, forthcoming.

Cuisenier, Jean. L'art populaire en France: rayonnement, modèles et sources. Fribourg, Switzerland: Office du livre, 1975.

Decorated Nova Scotia Furnishings. Halifax, N.S.: Dalhousie Art Gallery, 1978.

Dupont, Jean-Claude. "L'art populaire au Canada français". Pages 11–20 in Ethnologie québécoise, vol. 1. Compiled by Robert-Lionel Séguin. Montréal: Hurtubise HMH, 1972.

~ . Le sucre du pays. Montréal: Leméac, 1975.

An Exhibition of Canadian Gameboards of the Nineteenth and Twentieth Centuries from Ontario, Quebec and Nova Scotia. Halifax: Art Gallery of Nova Scotia, 1981.

Ferm, Vergilius. A Brief Dictionary of American Superstitions. New York: Philosophical Library, 1965.

Fillipetti, Hervé, and Trotereau, Janine. Symboles et pratiques rituelles dans la maison paysanne traditionnelle. Paris: Berger Levrault, 1978.

Folk Art in Canada. Plattsburg, N.Y.: Clinton County Historical Association, 1981.

Folk Art of Nova Scotia: a Travelling Exhibition of Twentieth-Century Folk Art of Nova Scotia. Halifax, N.S.: Art Gallery of Nova Scotia, 1977.

Folk Art Treasures of Quebec. Québec: Ministère des affaires culturelles, Direction des musées et centres d'exposition, 1980.

Folk Painters of the Canadian West. Ottawa: National Gallery of Canada, 1960.

Fraser, Antonia. A History of Toys. London: Weidenfeld and Nicholson, 1966.

Fried, Frederick, and Fried, Mary. America's Forgotten Folk Arts. New York: Pantheon, 1978.

Genêt, Nicole; Vermette, Luce; and Décarie-Audet, Louise. Les objets familiers de nos ancêtres. Montréal: Éditions de l'Homme, 1974.

Glassie, Henry H. "Folk Art". Pages 253–80 in Folklore and Folklife: an Introduction. Edited by Richard M. Dorson. Chicago: University of Chicago Press, 1972.

~ . Patterns in the Material Folk Culture of the Eastern United States. Philadelphia: University of Pennsylvania Press, 1969.

"Grass Roots Art". Artscanada, no. 138/139 (December 1969), full issue.

Grassroots Saskatchewan. Regina: Norman Mackenzie Art Gallery, 1976.

Grosbois, Louise de; Lamothe, Raymonde; and Nantel, Lise. Les patenteux du Québec. Montréal: Parti-Pris, 1974.

Grunfield, F.V., ed. *Games of the World*. New York: Ballantine, 1977.

Hansen, Hans Jurgen, ed. *European Folk Art in Europe and the Americas*. New York: McGraw-Hill, 1968.

Harper, J. Russell. "Folk Sculpture of Rural Quebec: the Nettie Sharpe Collection". *Antiques* 103 (April 1973): 724–33.

~ . *People's Art: Naïve Art in Canada*. Ottawa: National Gallery of Canada, 1973.

~ . *A People's Art: Primitive, Naïve, Provincial, and Folk Painting in Canada*. Toronto: University of Toronto Press, 1974.

Haselberger, Herta. "Method of Studying Ethnological Art". *Current Anthropology* 2 (1961): 341–84.

Hemphill, Herbert W., Jr., and Weissman, Julia. *Twentieth-Century American Folk Art and Artists*. New York: Dutton, 1974.

Hemphill, Herbert W., Jr., ed. *Folk Sculpture USA*. New York: Brooklyn Museum, 1976.

Hercík, Emanuel. *Folk-Toys*. Prague: Artia, 1951.

Hertz, Louis H. *The Toy Collector*. New York: Hawthorn, 1976.

Horwitz, Elinar Lander. *Contemporary American Folk Artists*. Philadelphia: Lippincott, 1975.

Inglis, Stephen. *Something Out of Nothing: the Work of George Cockayne*. National Museum of Man, Mercury Series. Canadian Centre for Folk Culture Studies Paper. Ottawa: National Museums of Canada, forthcoming.

Jacobs, Joseph. "The Folk". *Folklore* 4 (1893): 233–8.

Joe Sleep Retrospective. Halifax, N.S.: Art Gallery of Nova Scotia, 1981.

Jones, Michael Owen. "The Concept of 'Aesthetic' in the Traditional Arts". *Western Folklore* 30(2): 77–104.

~ . *A Feeling for Form, as Illustrated by People at Work*. Bloomington, Ind.: Trickster Press, 1980.

~ . *The Hand-Made Object and Its Maker*. Berkeley, Calif.: University of California Press, 1975.

Knowlson, Thomas Sharper. *The Origins of Popular Superstitions and Customs*. 1910. Reprint. Detroit: Gale Research, 1968.

Köngas-Maranda, Elli. "Les formes élémentaires de l'art folklorique". Pages 263-70 in *Mélanges en l'honneur de Luc Lacourcière: Folklore français d'Amérique*, edited by Jean-Claude Dupont. Montréal: Leméac, 1978.

Lacourcière, Luc. "Le destin posthume de la Corriveau". *Les cahiers des dix*, 34 (1969): 239–71.

Lessard, Michel. *Complete Guide to French-Canadian Antiques*. Translated by Elizabeth Abbott. New York: Hart, 1974.

Lessard, Michel, and Marquis, Huguette. *L'art traditionnel au Québec*. Montréal: Éditions de l'Homme, 1975.

Lévi-Strauss, Claude. *La pensée sauvage*. Paris: Plon, 1962.

Lichten, Frances. *Folk Art of Rural Pennsylvania*. New York: Scribner, 1946.

Lipman, Jean, and Winchester, Alice. *The Flowering of American Folk Art, 1776–1876*. New York: Viking Press, 1974.

McKendry, Ruth. *Quilts and Other Bed Coverings in the Canadian Tradition*. Toronto: Van Nostrand Reinhold, 1979.

Martinon, Jean-Pierre. "Les formes du pauvre". *Ethnologie française*, n.s. 8, nos. 2–3 (1978): 201–24.

Mattie, W.C. "Museum of Man Folk Art Collection". *Canadian Antiques and Art Review*, November 1979, pp. 26–31.

Metcalf, Harlan G. *Whittlin', Whistles and Thingamajigs: The Pioneer Book of Nature Crafts and Recreation*. Harrisburg Pa.: Stackpole Books, 1974.

Musée du Québec. *Le jouet dans l'univers de l'enfant, 1800–1925*. Québec: Ministère des affaires culturelles, 1977.

Pain, Howard. *The Heritage of Upper-Canadian Furniture: a Study in the Survival of Formal and Vernacular Styles from Britain, America and Europe, 1780–1900*. Toronto: Van Nostrand Reinhold, 1978.

Palardy, Jean. *Les meubles anciens du Canada français*. Paris: Art et Métiers graphiques, 1963.

Patterson, Nancy-Lou Gellermann. *Swiss-German and Dutch-German Mennonite Traditional Art in the Waterloo Region, Ontario*. National Museum of Man, Mercury Series. Canadian Centre for Folk Culture Studies, Paper No. 27. Ottawa: National Museums of Canada, 1979.

Pinto, Edward H. *Treen and Other Wooden Bygones*. London: G. Bell, 1969.

"Prairie Folk Art". *Artscanada*, no. 230/231 (October/November 1979), full issue.

Quimby, Ian M.G., and Swank, Scott T., eds. *Perspectives on American Folk Art*. New York: Norton, 1980.

Salaman, R.A. *Dictionary of Tools Used in the Woodworking and Allied Trades, c. 1700–1970*. New York: Scribner, 1977.

Séguin, Robert-Lionel. *Les moules du Québec*. National Museum of Canada, Bulletin 188. Ottawa: Queen's Printer, 1963.

Stoudt, John Joseph. *Pennsylvania German Folk Art*. Allentown, Pa.: Schechter's, 1966.

Tilney, Philip V.R. *Artifacts from the CCFCS Collections: Sampling No. 1*. National Museum of Man, Mercury Series. Canadian Centre for Folk Culture Studies, Paper No. 5. Ottawa: National Museums of Canada, 1973.

'Twas Ever Thus: A Selection of Eastern Canadian Folk Art. Toronto: Feheley, 1979.

Archival Materials Consulted from the Collection of the Canadian Centre for Folk Culture Studies

Jean-François Blanchette Collection
BJF-E-12, 13, 47. Interviews with Léon Ipperciel, Montebello, Qué., 1979 and 1980.
BJF-E-18 to 21, 35, 41, 43, 65 to 82. Interviews with Nelphas Prévost, Fassett, Qué., 1979 to 1981.
BJF-E-56, 57. Interviews with Noé J. Champagne, Bishopton, Qué., 1980.
BJF-E-63. Interview with John Robert Goyer, Brownsburg, Qué., 1981.
Canadian Broadcasting Corporation Collection (Donnalu Wigmore, Producer)
C.B.C.-B-M/4. Interviews in 1978 with:
Frank Kocevar, Kelowna, B.C.
Sam Spencer, Saskatoon, Sask.
Jeanne Thomarat, Duck Lake, Sask.
Cornelius Van Ieperen, Consul, Sask.
Bernie Wren, Langley, B.C.
Pierre Crépeau Collection
CRE-A-42 to 44. Interviews with Alfred Morneault, Edmundston, N.B., 1979.
Steve Delroy Collection
DEL-A-1 to 25. Interviews with Nettie Sharpe, Saint-Lambert, Qué., 1977.
Chris Huntington Collection
HUN-A-1. Interview with Albert Lohnes, West Berlin, N.S., 1975.
HUN-A-1, 2. Interviews with Ralph Boutilier, Milton, Queens County, N.S., 1975 and 1976.
HUN-A-3 (1, 2), 11. Interviews with Collins Eisenhauer, Union Square, N.S., 1975, 1976 and 1977.
HUN-A-8. Interview with Charlie Atkinson, South Side, Cape Sable Island, N.S., 1976.
Stephen Inglis Collection
ING-B-1 to 4. Interviews with George Cockayne, Madoc, Ont., 1981.
Wesley Mattie Collection
MAT-D-1. Interview with Sam Spencer, Saskatoon, Sask., 1979.

Index of Artists

The numbers are those assigned to the artifacts in the catalogue.

PHOTOGRAPHY

The majority of the photographs
are by Shin Sugino.

Harry Foster photographed the
frontispiece and the artifacts
numbered 2–10, 17–21, 24–28,
30–32, 34–40, 43, 54–56, 60, 62,
67–72, 75–76, 78–84, 86–88,
104–5, 108–10, 112, 114–16, 120,
123–4, 127, 129, 131, 133, 137,
139, 144, 149–60, 166, 171, 184–5,
188, 190–91, 194–6, 201, 206–7,
223, 225–6, 243–4, 249, 251,
254–6, and 260–70.

The photograph of No. 125 is
by John Corneil.

**Cover photographs by
Harry Foster**

EDITING
Viviane Appleton

PRODUCTION
James MacLeod

DESIGN
Frank Newfeld